Bob Moats

I0567278

FATAL

REJECTION

By Bob Moats

Rev. 0416140045

Fatal Rejection

ISBN - 978-0-9903138-8-5

For information and address:
Magic 1 Productions
P.O. Box 524, Fraser MI 48026-0524
Website: http://murdernovels.com
Cover by Bob Moats

My thanks to:

Val Brooks for her contributions to this book. She originally wrote the second chapter and gave me great ideas for the plot and the motivation to do it. I hope she continues to write for herself, she is very talented.

My gratitude to Sally Berneathy who re-edited this book in December 2012 and is editing some of my other books.

Thank you for purchasing this book, I hope you enjoy it as much as I enjoyed writing them for my faithful readers. Please feel free to email me to tell me what you thought about my stories. I can be reached at murdernovels@mail.com thanks again!

Advanced Reviews from the beta readers:

Bob Moats, the author of over 40 continuous "Murder" books, out did himself in "Fatal Rejection." This fiction book in a word is "intense". Derek Harcourt has written and had published a true crime book about the NY Slasher, a serial killer who was never caught. Before having his book published, he was rejected many times by publishing companies. Enter, Sarah Keller, an editor of a major publishing company in New York whose husband was murdered several months ago. She decided to start over and moved across country to Washington State. But, Harcourt has other plans for Sarah and commences to drive out to her. The book is full of heart stopping suspense with likeable characters and at times a little humor. Will Sarah find happiness away from her haunted past, or will her refusal letter to publish a mad man's book be a Fatal Rejection? I would give this book 5 stars.

R.J. Parker - Author of "Unsolved Serial Killers" and "Women who Kill"

Bob Moats once again amazes me with his brilliant storytelling ability. In "Fatal Rejection", he writes from the point of view of not only the victim but the murderer as well and he was able to pull it off wonderfully. The parts of the story told through the eyes of the victim, Sarah, were soft and light with a hint of sadness while the parts told through the murderer's eyes, Derek, were brash and hard and it was easy to get caught up in the characters. I thoroughly enjoyed this novel and found it difficult to put down.

Boni J. Rychener @bjrychener on Twitter

All finished. I enjoyed it. I liked that the ending was out of the blue as well. Very enjoyable and the ending was a good twist.

Dave, from England, @docbungle on Twitter.

The Author

Bob Moats is the author of 40 books about a senior citizen sleuth named Jim Richards, starting with the first book of the series, "Classmate Murders". He wrote the short fantasy novella "Crystal Prison of Kyr" and is a published playwright with his three act comedy "Happily Ever After". This book takes him to a new genre, serial killings and it views from two different perspectives, the killer and the victim.

"At any given time in the U.S. there are 35-50 active serial killers at work, continually changing their targets and methods. Serial murders are one of the most terrifying things that can happen to a community.

From "Unsolved Serial Killings - True Crimes" By R.J. Parker

Fatal Rejection

By Bob Moats

Chapter 1

The tears in Stacey Kimball's eyes stung. She couldn't wipe them away since her hands were tied with plastic zip ties to the sides of the straight back wood chair. They were cutting into her skin as she struggled to break free. She couldn't move her feet since her ankles were also tied to the chair.

She kept trying to blink the wetness from her eyes, but they kept filling. She tried to see the room she was in, but her glasses were gone and she was nearly blind without them. The tears occasionally would act like contact lenses, and she could sort of see where she was.

It was a dingy room. Smells of mold wafted through the air. Her gag reflex was growing, but her mouth was duct taped shut. She was helpless all around. When she could see, the walls were dark, dirty looking bricks, and the floor seemed to be dirt. It must be a cellar somewhere in Pelham, New York, she thought. That was the last city she knew she was in, so she assumed she was still there.

The last thing she remembered was bending into the trunk of her car, putting in groceries, when she suddenly felt a hot stinging at the back of her neck. Then everything went black. She awoke tied to the chair and realized she must have been tasered, but by whom? And why the hell her? She was helpless and didn't like the feeling. Her hate for the situation was growing inside her. She wanted the person who did this to die.

The tears still stung, and she was holding on to her gag reflex, not wanting to drown in her vomit. She couldn't imagine who'd want to do this to her. Had she pissed off someone so badly that she ended up in a stinking cellar, possibly to die there, never to be found? The tears flowed worse now. She tried to shake her head to clear her eyes, but it didn't work.

She listened to the room. It was totally quiet, no sound at all. Then it came.

The sound of a door opening behind and above her. A sliver of light struck the floor. Her terror rose. Was it time to face her attacker?

Fatal Rejection

Foot sounds were advancing down what she believed to be stairs—thump... thud... thump... thud... it continued until they reached the dirt. Stacey was wetting her pants. The person stayed behind her, but she felt the presence close, too close.

She stiffened slightly against her bindings when she felt fingers on her earlobes. They started to caress her lobes, giving her shivers. Her gag reflex stepped up a notch. The man rubbed slowly around her ears, causing a tingle in her stomach. She hated it and the person doing it.

The man brought his hands down to her blouse and pulled at the front, causing it to open. He pulled the blouse down around her shoulders, exposing the breasts in her bra. He brought his hands slowly down to her ample breasts and slid them into the cups of her bra. The tingle in her stomach increased, her breath heightened as he moved around her nipples. This was not how it should be.

The bastard was pushing and pulling at her breasts. It hurt. She wanted to scream but couldn't. Then he stopped.

She felt her hair being pulled back, forcing her to face the ceiling, hurting her neck. She wondered if he even cared. His face came over hers. She could see him now. He had a plain face, dark hair, mustache and deep brown eyes. Under other circumstances she might have liked him, found him handsome even. But

8

this bastard was controlling her, making her feel worse than she had ever felt.

She wanted to scream, "What do you want?" but the tape held her mute. He suddenly ripped the tape from her mouth She gasped for air. The air was stale and putrid tasting, but she still took a deep breath.

"What the fuck do you want, you son of a bitch?" she screamed.

He came around and faced her. He still looked good enough to date, but her revulsion for him intensified.

"Stacey, you need to relax. I don't want you upset when I kill you," he said quietly, as though he were ordering a happy meal at McDonalds.

Her mouth dropped open and she couldn't speak. Choking sounds came from her throat. "Who are you and why me?" she finally got out.

"Oh, Stacey, you are so much like all the rest, the women who tried to screw me over, ruin my life. You are just one of many like them that I will take the life out of. You aren't the first."

The man went back around her and pulled her head back again, slitting her throat with a large knife he pulled from a sheath on his belt. The blood sprayed. He waited till it subsided and then came around her and looked close into her eyes.

"I love seeing the life going out of a person. Die bitch," he said softly. Then when the life drained from her, he whispered, "Be happy knowing that you won't be the last."

~~*~~

Derek Harcourt sat back in his ergonomic desk chair and stared at the screen of the laptop. He had just finished writing about the death of Stacy Kimball, the latest chapter of the new book he was working on. He was thinking about the next murder that the serial killer would commit. This was all so easy.

He sat quietly looking around his room where he was working on his second novel. He glanced at the book shelves, seeing all the books he had read many times. One whole shelf was dedicated to just one book, his first.

He put his head back on the chair and remembered the pains he had gone through to get that book published. He spent nearly two years putting it together from extensive research of his favorite serial killer, one who had never been caught. Derek admired the man, so much so that he dedicated his first book to him.

When he had finished writing the book he sent submissions out to as many agents and publishers as he could find and then waited. He still had a box full of the rejection slips that came flowing back into his mail slot. Then one day he received that letter from an editor at a New York publishing firm asking him to send his full manuscript to her. He was ecstatic. He wrapped the pages carefully and delivered them to the post office, sending them off. He waited almost three weeks, agonizing over what they would say. Then the day came that he received the letter. Tearing into it, he read.

She tore his book apart, citing all the errors and misplaced plot lines, no cohesive structure or even a thread of sense concerning the man the book was about. She regretted wasting Derek's time, but they couldn't use it as submitted, even with extreme editing.

He nearly fell to the floor in tears as he read the words the woman had written.

Derek spent the next week in a haze. His health deteriorated, and he hardly ate. He had counted so much on that one publisher, the only one who expressed interest. To be so brutally disappointed hurt terribly.

Fatal Rejection

Then one night his rage grew and he made a vow to polish up his book and get it checked before trying to submit again. He gathered what money he had and borrowed what he could to hire a professional editor who worked with him until it was ready.

For the next two months he personally hand-delivered the book to the publishers in New York. His perseverance finally paid off. He had an interested company who read his book and liked it. He signed the standard contracts and the book was on its way.

Book releases don't happen overnight. It took time to get his book ready and printed then out to the stores. He was finally receiving good reviews, and sales started to grow. His book made the charts, not high up but at least he was on the charts, and he finally felt the glory of his efforts. But he never forgot the pain he went through to get there.

He never forgot or forgave that one editor and her criticisms, but he had triumphed over her words and become a successful writer.

He came back from his thoughts and saved the chapter that he had just written. He attached it to the email he was sending off to the editor he had chosen for his new book. She was a woman who lived out in Washington state.

Now he would start on a new chapter and a new murder.

*

Chapter 2

It was the perfect house for her new start, Sarah thought as she knelt on the floor to unpack boxes in her new bedroom. The octagonally designed home sat in its own cul-de-sac at the top of a rolling hill that ended in the cool waters of the Hood Canal. The strange shape of the place lent it its own personality. That suited Sarah just fine as she had always been considered a bit of an oddball herself. None of her friends could understand why Sarah wanted to move out to the woods and live by herself. After all she had gone through, they thought she needed to build her strength with a wall of people who never left her alone. It was difficult to cope with the deaths and betrayal, and she just wanted to escape.

After taking several weeks leave from her job at Scheuler Publishing, she returned thinking she could throw herself into her work. It was the only escape for her in the city. She loved editing, loved being drawn into the author's writing as the various tales unfolded before her. Fiction was her favorite genre, but her love of books in general allowed her to be captivated in almost any field. Only things didn't quite work out how she planned. She couldn't quite seem to get back into the swing of things, found herself distracted constantly whether by the various horde of people "checking" on her or her own inability to focus on her work. Sarah felt trapped, and the hurried life of the city seemed to compound her aggression, her anger, and her stress. Sean's murder had induced paranoia to form in her brain. She never felt secure, never felt safe anymore. A locksmith had come and installed extra locks at her request, but even those, she felt, couldn't keep anyone out.

After seven months of being back at work, Sarah was ready to walk out. She told her associate, Connie, another editor at Scheuler, that she was thinking of moving away. She had been perusing secluded properties online and had found a house that appealed to her in Washington, the state. Connie was dumbstruck by the revelation. Sarah was one of the best editors in the business. The girl had an eye for detail and for what would sell on the market. She was an asset to the company, and Connie knew they wouldn't want to lose her.

"Becoming a crazy hermit lady is not the way to go, Sarah," Connie had told her. Connie was happy to live out her existence in the single world, being dubbed "the party girl" and having one night stands with the cutest guy she could find at her chosen watering hole - and she got wet in a lot of places. Connie felt sure that Sarah would recover from her trauma much faster by releasing her inner demons on unsuspecting men. "Just use them, honey. They don't mind, really. Most of them are just looking for a good time themselves. Everyone has troubles they want to forget about for a while," Connie said. That had never been a lifestyle Sarah could accept. Her Catholic upbringing probably had a lot to do with it, and the truth of the matter was that she missed Sean and her heart was broken. She wasn't ready to just forget her troubles. She knew she had to deal with them head-on.

"Con, I really need this. I'm going crazy here. My life changed when Sean died. It's not coming back to me here. At least not right now," Sarah said, pleading her case to her friend. She knew she would be sacrificing one of the most prominent positions in the publishing world and leaving behind a life she had built for herself. It took dedication and hard work to finally reach her goals, and she knew she was throwing it all away. Sometimes people needed new goals, she rationalized with herself.

"Honey, your emotions are in over-drive right now. What about your job? This is where you belong, not out in the woods with some 'Deer Hunter' types. Let me hear you squeal like a pig…" They both laughed at Connie's attempt at movie quotes.

"That's 'Deliverance,' Connie, and I promise if I hear banjoes playing, I'll run like crazy," Sarah said jokingly. "I figure I can edit from home as an independent. So I won't be completely out of the loop. Maybe I'll go and find I can't stand it, but as it is, the thought of having some privacy, some peace and quiet, sounds like the best thing in the world to me. Fresh air, Con. No honking horns, no traffic jams, no crowded streets. Ever since Sean died, I feel, well, I'm scared now. Some days I swear I can feel someone watching me. I look around and all the faces blend together. I'm really freaking out here."

Connie ran her hands over her mocha colored face, trying to erase the stress of the situation. "Sarah, I don't see how I can stop you unless I chain you to your desk. That never makes for a good employee relationship. I don't want you to go, but I do want you to be okay. I just don't see how it will do any good for you to isolate yourself from the world. I also know you don't want to hear this, but you will recover from this and you'll move on. Sean wasn't the last man on earth, you know." Sarah bristled at the comment. Connie held up her hand. "Just listen, please. You are young, you are beautiful, and men will want you, baby. I know you think you don't want anyone right now, but you'll get lonely. It happens, that's life."

"Maybe so. Right now I just need to get away. There are too many memories here. Every time I walk into our bedroom, all I see is the blood and the bodies. I can't sleep, I can't eat. I've got to do something." Tears welled up in Sarah's eyes and fell down her cheeks.

"Most people would just see a shrink, but, oh no, not you. You've got to go run out to the woods and play Grizzly Adams." Connie sighed. "Fine, I get it. Maybe we can see about you staying on. Files can be sent electronically these days, so no biggie there. Hal's just old fashioned and likes to have an office full of people. Let me talk to him and see what we can work out."

"Thanks, Connie," Sarah said, wiping her eyes with a wad of tissue.

Three months after that conversation with Connie, Sarah found herself flying out to Washington to sign the papers with the real estate agency and making arrangements to move her belongings. She said farewell to her friends at work during a party they threw for her and headed to the Northwest. The real estate agent, Lois Carter, was kind enough to have the power turned on and a phone line hooked up for Sarah's arrival.

"You'll just need to go down to the power company and sign their agreement in person. Then you'll be all set," Lois said when she met Sarah at the house. Sarah thanked the lady and went to work on unpacking, arranging and trying to make design plans for her new home. Digging through one of the boxes, she came across her favorite photo of her and Sean. His arms wrapped around her from behind, and they were both smiling. Sarah sighed deeply. God, how she missed him. It just wasn't fair.

Fatal Rejection

They had planned to have a family together, had just a bought a four bedroom home and started renovations, including a baby nursery. Sarah had quit taking her birth control pills, too. They both felt the time had come, and she had been excited at the prospect of being pregnant and having babies with the man she loved. Their careers were on the upswing, she an editor for one of the largest publishing houses in the country, he an artist. Sean's first gallery showing happened two months before his death. Every one of his paintings sold and the gallery had started pushing him for more. Two weeks after his death someone from the Jadite Galleries called. "Mrs. Keller, this is Samuel Jones. We send our deepest condolences to you and your family. What happened to Sean was tragic. We're all still reeling from the news here."

Sarah knew what the call was about. She'd fully expected it. Even though her life seemed to hit a brick wall and come to a complete stop, the world still moved on around her. A part of her wanted to be angry at Mr. Jones for the intrusive phone call, but she knew her anger wasn't directed at the man. He had a job to do, and Sarah was sure the phone call wasn't a high point in his day either. She took a deep breath, composing her thoughts before she spoke. "Thank you, Mr. Jones. It was a shock for everyone."

"Yes, yes…a shock indeed. And I'm sorry to call and bother you, but the gallery wanted you to know that, if you find yourself needing a representative for any of Sean's work, we will be happy to help you in any way we can. His exhibition was one of the most successful we've ever had. He was a rare talent, Mrs. Keller. People are still calling several times a week asking for more of his work. I don't imagine you would be ready to release any of his paintings at this time, but as I said, we just want you to know we are here."

"Thank you, Mr. Jones, for supporting Sean. I'm still sorting through everything." Sarah had to work to hold back her tears and her anger. "When or if I should decide to let go of anything, you will be the first person I will call." She wanted the conversation to end and couldn't stand the thought of selling anything of Sean's.

"Thank you, Mrs. Keller. And once again, our condolences to you." Mr. Jones hung up the telephone, relieved that Sean's wife was cordial, considering the circumstances. At the other end of the line, Sarah replaced the handset into its base and broke down. Her grief washed over her in waves making her feel as if she would drown in her own pain.

They were happy, or so she thought. Now any hope of those dreams was obliterated and Sean was gone forever. "You've got to stop thinking about it, stop living in the past," Sarah said to herself. "You need to heal." That's what Washington was about—

healing. A movement caught her attention through one of the many floor-to-ceiling windows in her bedroom. She got up from her knees and slowly made her way to the glass. A doe stood right outside her bedroom window accompanied by a fragile looking fawn. Sarah couldn't help but smile at the sight. Yes, this was going to be perfect!

*

Chapter 3

His real name was Eugene Petrovskia, but at the insistence of his publisher, he took on the name Derek Harcourt. The publisher felt his real name was too hard to remember and sounded too foreign for readers to want his book. Derek Harcourt sounded more like an author on a roll, and it paid off. People were buying his first book, and the reviewers were kind.

He didn't like using a pen name as he wouldn't be known by former so-called friends and family as a soon-to-be famous author. He told himself that one day he would write letters to everyone he knew, explaining that it was good old Eugene from Bishop High School in Detroit who had a book in stores, the same Eugene everyone tormented for being a nerd. He hated those people and that was why he put off informing them of his success.

Bob Moats

Both of his parents were closet drunks, hiding bottles from each other and fighting about their location. They would find any reason to fight, and Eugene would hide in his room to avoid being hit by a flying lamp or toaster. His mother gave up one day and killed herself, hanging from the front porch so all the world could see, making Eugene the butt of new jokes. His father drank even heavier then, and a fed up Eugene packed a few things and left.

An eighteen year old alone on the streets of Detroit was not a smart thing to do. But he survived by his wits and imagination. He got a job in a deli, sweeping floors and cleaning the meat grinders of all the blood and gristle. That part made him gag, but he held on. The store owner let him live in the basement because he felt sorry for the boy and he wanted someone in the store to watch it after closing.

Eugene would sit in his dank make shift room, reading crime magazines that the deli store had on a magazine rack upstairs to sell. He was fascinated by the stories they told, and he became interested in one particular serial killer they called the NY Slasher. The killer had never been caught and slashed his way across the United States, murdering over 30 women. Then he just disappeared.

Eugene was also fascinated by words, the words he read in the magazines and a few books he picked up in a local book store, all crime novels. He felt, with his new knowledge from the crime magazines and his desire to write, some day he would be a famous author.

His desire to become a writer was put on hold. He became involved with a local gang and ended up being caught when they tried to rob a local party store. One of the gang members shot a police officer and killed him. All of the five members of the gang were arrested, and Eugene went to prison for being involved in a death related shooting during a robbery. He was released after ten years and decided not to go back to Detroit. He went east to New York and hooked up with a woman he was corresponding with through an online pen-pal service for prisoners. He found she wasn't what she pretended to be online. She was really fat and loud, but he needed a place to stay so he endured living with her.

He managed to get a job in a factory making plastic parts for different automotive products and was working long hours, mostly to make money but also to get away from the woman. He would often go to the local library and use their computers to work on a book. The library had a wealth of information on the subject he wanted to write about—serial killers. He became absorbed in the subject and would frequently be asked to leave so the library could close.

He managed to purchase a cheap computer to use at home, and he immersed himself in the book. The woman he lived with finally moved out to live with a man twice her age who had money. She didn't need the piss poor living conditions they had, so she left. Eugene was glad to see her go. Now he could concentrate on his story.

Two years later he finished the story. He had no idea about the publishing world and how it worked. He read books about it and they all said you needed an agent or publisher. So he sent out his manuscript and was rejected for every one he sent out. Then he received that one letter asking for his full manuscript, and he sent it to the woman who was an editor for a New York Publisher.

Derek Harcourt sat back trying to forget the pain he went through during that turning point in his life. His determination finally got him into a publishing firm, despite what that female editor said in her cruel letter. He wouldn't forget her. His new publisher changed his name. Eugene Petrovskia was dead, murdered by his success as a writer. He was now Derek Harcourt, author extraordinaire.

~~*~~

"What the hell do you mean, you're going to travel the country?" Ken Rawlings yelled at Derek from across his huge desk, sitting in the hot seat as

Fatal Rejection

Ken called it. Rawlings was Derek's publisher and acted as his agent.

"I plan on following in the footsteps of the NY Slasher to get a feel for the man," Derek replied.

"But you already wrote about him. This book isn't about him. You told me it was a new thriller about a different serial killer. That's what you said and what I'm banking our money on. Don't tell me you really need to run around the country to write your book."

"Ken, I need to get my head into this and if I visit places where his murders took place, I can add some realism to it. Yes, it's a new killer. I need to develop him into what the NY Slasher was, only more evil. I'll be going from New York all the way to Seattle."

"Seattle? Why there?"

"I've always wanted to go to Seattle, maybe to get an original Starbucks coffee. What can I say? It's part of my book. You'll love it."

"Hey, isn't your new editor somewhere in Washington State? The one you want to use instead of our in-house editors?"

"Yes, and I plan to visit her. We've only met through e-mails and an occasional phone call. I want to meet her face to face finally."

"Whatever. Just get the book done. I'll be on your ass if you're late."

"Not to worry, Ken, I'll get it to you. I'll have it done by your deadline."

"That's six months away. You better move on it.

"Don't worry, I'll have it to you, and you'll love the ending of this book. I guarantee." Derek smiled and stood. "Now I have packing to do, so I'll be in touch." He turned and went out the office door.

"You better, or you're finished in this business," Ken yelled after him.

Derek thought to himself, "I just may be finished after this trip."

*

Chapter 4

Sarah awoke early the next morning, feeling a little better and ready to finish putting her things into place. Most of her boxes that had been delivered by the moving company still sat around getting in the

Fatal Rejection

way. She had put off finishing the job mostly because she felt odd being in the new house without Sean. Her dreams had crumbled the night he died, but she was going to try and make a new start in the small town she moved to from across the country. It was far from the life she had in New York. She slowly dragged herself to the kitchen to make breakfast, but started to tear up again. She was doing a lot of that. Sean was always the person to make breakfast. Sarah had no talent for cooking.

She went to the refrigerator, looked at the few items of food she had, and realized she needed to do some shopping. Not something she wanted to do alone in a strange town. In New York you could get lost in the crowd, and she always had Sean with her. She realized that she might not be able to survive without Sean, but she had to rise up and make an effort to get on with her new life.

It was damp and chilly out that morning. She got her jacket from the vestibule rack and put it on. She paused at the full length windows in the living room looking out to the Hood Canal. The sight was still breathtaking even after seeing it every day since she moved in. She stood watching the sea gulls doing their aerobatics and diving for fish. This is something you don't see in the big city, she thought.

She picked up the keys to her new car and went to the front door. She had purchased the Chevy Vibe on the second day she was in her new home town. In

Bob Moats

New York City you could get just about anywhere without a car, so she and Sean had opted not to get one. In Brinnon you had to have a car as everything was so spaced out you could have a heart attack trying to walk anywhere. The central part of the town was about five miles from her home. She had only driven through it once, the day she bought the car. Luckily, the real estate agent she had was very helpful in getting her set up. Sarah liked Lois although the woman was in her sixties. She was friendly and a seemingly kind person, but most people in small towns were that way, or so she heard. Now she would find out.

Sarah drove out the long driveway from her home to the highway and turned right onto the asphalt in the direction of town. The trees were in abundance there, mainly because it was a wet coastal area. The rain wasn't as bad as people made it out to be. Yes, there were a lot of misty days, but there were also sunny days. The impression of the Seattle area was lots of rain, but the mountain ranges protected the city from too many heavy, steady rains. The pavement today was wet but too not hazardous.

She drove the 101 North towards town to look for a place to buy groceries. She regretted not picking Lois' brain for more facts about the area, but she could always call her if she got lost or confused. At the corner of the 101 and a side street called Sylopash Lane was a building with a sign saying it was the

Fatal Rejection

Brinnon General Store. She pulled in and parked on the side.

She entered the building and saw it would serve her purpose for food relief. She took a cart and walked around, pulling things off the shelves, hoping they were something she would need. Next time she would make a grocery list, she thought. She came around the back of one aisle and saw her realtor Lois talking to a man in a police uniform. Lois glanced over and saw Sarah. She waved and called to her.

"Sarah! Come over here," she said.

Sarah pushed the cart to them and smiled at the handsome officer. "Hi, Lois. I was just trying to stock my kitchen even though I don't know what I need," Sarah said with a slight giggle.

"Oh, it will all come together, dear. You're just setting up, and it takes time to get it right. Sarah, this is Davis Chandler, our sheriff. Dave, this is Sarah Keller from New York. She's our new addition to town."

"Well, our population just went from 1197 to 1198. Pleased to meet you, Sarah, if I can call you Sarah?"

"Of course. I would never argue with a cop, if I can call you a cop." She laughed.

"Was that the respect you gave law enforcement in New York?"

"They usually were called pigs or other unsavory names, but I respect all law enforcement. Good to meet you." Sarah held her hand out, and the sheriff took it gently. His hand was warm and soft, not what she expected of a cop.

"Lois is the local town gossip, so I have heard a bit about you already. I'm sorry about your husband. Life isn't fair is it?" he said, then changed the subject. "Are you all settled in your new home?

"No, but I have made a dent in it. It's a wonderful home, very unique in its design."

"Yes, the house used to belong to a young couple named Carlson. The husband was an architect and designed the place himself. Based on an octagon, lots of big windows so the sun can come in, when there is a sun. They lived here about two years before moving over to Seattle to be closer to his work. The drive from here to Seattle is a killer around all the lakes. Lois also tells me you are a book editor."

"Is there anything you don't already know about me?" she said with a glance at Lois.

"Now, dear, I have to keep the sheriff informed of anything going on around the county. He likes to keep on top of things," Lois said with a sly smile.

Fatal Rejection

"Yes, Sheriff, I edit books for a company out in New York. It's always been a passion of mine, words."

"That sounds fascinating. You edit by e-mail, I presume?"

"Yes, I do. It took a bit of bribery to get the cable company to install the Internet at the house. I'm surprised the former owners didn't have it."

"The Carlsons were busy people and didn't have much time to watch TV or play on the Internet."

"Well, the Internet is my life connection. It makes working at home so much easier."

"Now if I could figure how to do my job from home, but the criminals would run rampant." The sheriff laughed.

"Are there many criminals around these parts?"

"My biggest bust on any one day is some tourist driving a little too fast through town. Not much in the way of New York crime here."

"Good, I am glad for that," she said, thinking about the murder of her husband and her best friend. She took a breath and tried not to start tearing up.

"It's good to meet you, Sheriff. Now I need to finish my shopping."

"Please call me Dave. We're not real formal here," he said.

"Well, call me Sarah then." She looked at Lois. "Good to see you again. I may need some advice on where everything is in town. May I call you?"

"Certainly, dear, call anytime. I know where everything is and the cheapest way to survive."

She thanked both of them and went back to shopping. After she returned home, she put everything in its place in the kitchen.

She went to her laptop to see what had arrived for her to work on. It would help take her mind off the unpacking. She booted up the computer and opened the e-mail program, reading what had come in.

Hal, her boss back in New York, said she could continue working for him. He didn't want to lose his best editor. She filed away the three manuscripts she received so she could check them later. Then saw the one from a very strange author back in New York. His name was Derek Harcourt, and he had only one book published. For some reason, he asked her to edit his newest book, and he was paying her well and under the table. She hadn't read his first book. She didn't want to get any preconceived ideas about his writing since that book was edited by someone else.

She opened his e-mail and read it. The subject made her skin crawl. She had edited murder novels before, but serial killers creeped her out. The death of her husband was blamed on a serial killer, so she almost refused to edit this man's book. But he offered her a good deal of money, so she took it despite her feelings on the subject. She read the words and not the subject, looking for errors or grammar problems. If she saw a sentence that confused her or made no sense, she noted it in the empty lines. She spent about an hour on it and finished. She filed it to send back later and went to make lunch.

She had bought bread and jelly but she really wanted a good ham sandwich. Next time in town she would see if she could find a deli and get some good cold cuts. If this town even had a deli. New York had a deli on just about every corner. She was starting to miss New York but this was her new home now and she would just have to make do. She didn't miss the traffic, the noise or the crime.

She wondered if she would get bored here.

*

Chapter 5

Buffalo, New York. Two days after Derek Harcourt last talked to his publisher, he arrived in Buffalo and drove to his motel. It was basically a dive, but that's what he wanted, to walk in the shoes of the NY Slasher and his quest to murder women across the country. He relaxed in the room, getting his laptop ready to start a new chapter. Thankfully this dive had Wi-Fi so he could hook up to the Internet and his mail provider. He checked his e-mail and found a reply from his editor in Washington, Sarah. His latest chapter was checked and corrected. He trusted her to make the right decisions. Or he hoped she would.

He read the e-mail and was satisfied with her corrections. There was not much to complain about. Since his first book he had learned a lot about writing so he self-edited his work before sending it on to her. He didn't want to tax her too early, not until he got to the climax of the book. It would be a killer finish.

He was tired from the long ride across New York State so he decided to take a quick nap. He set the alarm on his travel clock to wake him in an hour, enough time to recharge his internal battery. He fell on the bed. It sagged in the middle, probably from too many couples doing the dirty deed. The bed had an odd smell, about what you'd expect for a cheap motel. They probably rented by the hour, too.

An hour later his alarm went off. Derek stirred from his nap and sat on the edge of the bed, shaking the webs from his head. He had a lousy dream about being trapped in a room full of rats. He had hated rats ever since he was a child and the rats ran free through his home in Detroit. They were disgusting and would eat their food if it wasn't sealed and put up. Usually his dead drunken mother would leave their food out, a welcome gesture to the filthy, furry rodents.

Derek wanted to talk to the local police about the Slasher's adventures in Buffalo so he changed clothes and left the motel. He arrived at the police station and went in to the front desk where he waited for the officer to finish writing in a large book. The cop looked up at Derek and gave him a frown.

"Yeah, what's your problem?" he asked.

"No problem, officer. I just would like to talk to a detective about the NY Slasher. Could you tell me who I might talk to?"

"NY Slasher? I haven't heard that name in a number of years. Why you bringing it up?" He stood tall now, about six-four and nasty looking.

"I'm an author, writing a book about serial killers. The NY Slasher is a focal point of my latest book, research you might say."

"Your name?"

"Derek Harcourt."

The officer cracked a slight smile. "Yeah, Mr. Harcourt, I've read your book. I'll get a detective to talk to you." He picked up a phone and hit a couple buttons, listened, then asked for Detective Flint. He waited then explained what he had. He hung up and said, "Wait here. Detective Flint will be here shortly."

"Thank you," Derek said and went to a bench to sit. About ten minutes later a large man in a crumpled suit came out and motioned Derek to follow him. He led Derek to a small cubicle and asked him to sit.

"Now what do you want, Mr. Harcourt? I've have read your book. It wasn't bad, but I felt it glorified the NY Slasher. Not a good thing."

"Well, I did admire his guts to pull off the crimes and not get caught. The police and FBI to this day still don't have him in custody, do they?"

"No, they don't, but I believe he's dead. It's been too many years since he did his last killing out in California. Yes, he went through here in Buffalo. It wasn't something we wanted to talk about. When a serial killer is in the wind, we can't catch him if he's moving around fast and loose." The detective lifted his phone and asked for a file on the Slasher's murder in the city. He hung up, and then the detective questioned Derek about his book. About twenty minutes later an officer arrived with a folder and handed it to Flint.

"Mr. Harcourt, we normally don't do this, but I'm making an exception for such a distinguished author. Here's the folder on the murder here in Buffalo that we assumed was committed by the Slasher. Go across the hall to that room and you can go through it. Just return it to me when you are done."

Derek thanked him, took the file to the small room and read the contents, taking notes in the moleskin notebook he carried.

He finished an hour later and returned the file then left the station to drive back to his motel.

~~*~~

The woman was spread eagle, naked on the bed, arms and legs tied to the bed posts and duct tape across her mouth. She was sobbing behind the duct tape but no sounds came forth. The man moved over to her and sat on the bed next to her, moving his hands across her exposed breasts. She convulsed on

36

the bed causing the man to slap her hard on the face. She stopped moving.

"Now, now, Beth, you don't want to make this harder, do you?" he said. She stared through tear filled blood shot eyes and made no move to acknowledge him. She looked to her right, away from him, and shut her eyes. The man grabbed her face and pulled it back towards him. "Look at me, do you hear me!?" he yelled causing the woman to give him a panicked look.

"Better. Now just keep watching me." He stood and removed all his clothes as Beth watched, afraid to take her eyes off him. She felt the revulsion at the possibility of being raped by the now naked man.

He came back to her after putting his clothing in a plastic bag and sealing it. He sat again next to her and picked up a large knife from the bed stand where he had placed it earlier. He placed the sharp edge of the knife to her throat and slowly pulled it across. He didn't push hard, just enough to break the skin, causing her to bleed slowly from the cut.

"Oh, Beth, it is so beautiful to see the blood flow from your neck, like a little stream flowing in the forest. Only it's a red stream and we aren't in a forest now, are we?"

She felt the pain from the cut and was hyper-ventilating through her nose. She was ready to pass out when the man slapped her again. "Don't pass out on me, I won't allow it. I want to see you die. I want to see the life flow out of you. So don't pass out." He cut her throat deeper, causing blood to spurt out from her arteries, splattering his body. He took his hands and rubbed the blood all over his chest and arms, laughing and enjoying the feel of the warm liquid. The woman took a last breath through her nose and died.

The man stood and wiped the knife on the bed sheets then went to the bathroom to shower, making sure every bit of evidence was washed down the drain. He left the water running to be sure all was in the sewer. He returned to the room, removed his clothes from the plastic bag and dressed. He stood looking at her lifeless body then cut off a big lock of hair from Beth's still head. He put the hair in a plastic bag and slipped it into his pocket.

At the door to the motel he turned one last time to see his handiwork. Proud of his accomplishment, he took a couple pictures with his cell phone, just for the fun of it. He opened the door, being careful of watching eyes. He saw no one in the yard, and the security cameras had been disabled earlier by him so there was no evidence of his exit. He left and drove off, satisfied with his evening.

~~*~~

Derek had finished writing his latest chapter based on what he learned from the file in Flint's folder. He attached the chapter to the e-mail and sent it to Sarah for her expert opinion. Not that he cared. He would re-edit it again when he got the reply. He sent the mail and then went to the television, clicking through the five channels on the antique set. He stopped on the news and sat back watching the reporter talking about a murder in the city. Buffalo didn't have a lot of murders so even one was breaking news. He listened to the woman reporting on the scene.

"I'm talking to Officer Davis, Buffalo police, about the murder. Can you tell the viewers what happened?"

"Well, Linda, you know we can't talk about an ongoing investigation," he replied.

"I heard some talk from the first responders that this looked like the work of the NY Slasher. Could he be back?"

"Again, Linda, I can't comment on this until we have more information. Check with us tomorrow." He walked away from her, and she turned to the camera and started to talk, but Derek shut the TV off.

He sat thinking, "I need to get my alibi together and call Flint. I'm sure they'll want to talk to me."

*

Chapter 6

Sarah had finished as much as she was going to do for the day. She stood looking out at the vast body of water by the railing that kept people from accidentally wandering off the land's edge into the Hood Canal. She was mesmerized by the lake. She had never been near any large body of water in her life, having grown up in Albany, New York. She never went down to see the Atlantic Ocean on her few visits to New York City. When she married Sean, they moved to the city, but again she stayed mostly within the city. She wondered why she had always avoided the water before.

She turned back towards the house and heard a car coming up the drive. It was always so quiet out there, the sound of a car brought back memories, the hustle and bustle of New York and the traffic congestion that deafened the ears. She no longer missed it.

She went towards the car and saw it was Lois. She greeted her as Lois opened her door, struggling with her attempt at getting out of the car.

"Damn, as you get old, even exiting a car can be a chore. My advice is, never grow old." She laughed. Sarah liked Lois' laugh. It was pleasant and friendly.

"I'll keep that in mind. What brings you out here?" Sarah asked.

"A bit of gossip," she said with a sly smile. "Sheriff Dave was taken with you. I think he may even like you."

"Lois, it's a little premature to be hooking me up with anyone. I'm still in mourning."

"Dear, it's been almost a year. Don't you think it's time to start your life up again?"

"It's been only seven months. How long is a good period for mourning?"

"Well, there are a couple of ladies in town who got back in the saddle within months of their spouse's demise."

"I'm not taking riding lessons, Lois. I have loved my husband since the day we met, and I don't want to lose his memory."

Fatal Rejection

"Of course not, dear. But a woman alone shouldn't be alone. Words of wisdom from an old lady who's been there."

"You never mentioned if you're married, Lois."

"Oh hell, no. I was married three times. Now I just live with Harold, my younger boyfriend. He's fifty-eight, I'm sixty-two. I'm what you call a cougar. I gave up on marriage long ago, too confining. I can kick Harold out anytime he displeases me." She laughed, causing Sarah to laugh with her.

"You're not exactly a great ad for the sanctity of wedlock," Sarah said.

"You mean deadlock. I think all women should ride the horse a while before buying it. Oh, there I go again making equestrian jokes. I don't know why. I dislike horses. Now back to your problem. Dave is a good catch. You should look into him. He's a free agent now that his girlfriend moved to Seattle."

"They broke up?"

"Well, she was never right for him. Good thing she left town. She was such a flighty woman, always arguing about the stupidest things with Dave. I'm surprised he put up with her for so long."

"How long has she been gone?"

"About a month. I think Dave is being cautious. There are any number of ladies in town who would like to harness him. Again with the horse references. I don't know what's wrong with me today."

"Well, he won't have to worry about me. I'm not interested. Although he was good looking," Sarah said, "I need a little more time to adjust to all this. I've only been here a month. I still need to get used to country life."

"Yes, my dear, you need to settle down. A nice young man would help with that."

"You just aren't going to let it go, are you?"

"Of course not, dear. I'm the head of the local busybodies in this county."

She laughed and went back to her car, opened the door then turned back to Sarah. "Let me know if you would like to get to know Dave better. I can arrange it for you." She got in the car before Sarah had time to respond. She waved and started the car, driving back out the drive.

Sarah winced as she watched the older woman speed away. If this is what country living does to you, Sarah thought, she would just stay inside her home.

Fatal Rejection

She went back into the living room and to the corner where she had her computer set up on a desk facing the water. She could see that she had a couple messages from her mail program. She sat, opened up the program and saw that her friend, Connie, had sent her a message. She opened it and read.

"Sarah, how's everything out in the woods? Seen any bears or good looking lumberjacks yet? Nothing's changed here, still boring. Hal is grumpy since you left, although it's good you still communicate with us by sending in your edits. I met a really great guy the other night. He's an investment broker and wealthy. The kind of man I like. Nothing serious for now. You know me, I'm never serious. We had a good time partying and going out to the theater. He also has season tickets to the opera. I hate the opera, but I'm going for him. I've dragged him to a couple clubs in the city. He's a good dancer but he does stumble occasionally. I hope you're meeting people, going to bingo or a quilting bee. Are you churning your own butter yet? God, I miss you. I'll try and get out your way one day, then we can both run around the woods looking for hot lumberjacks. Take care, Connie."

Sarah smiled and closed the e-mail. She'd reply later. She looked at the other e-mail. It was from creepy writer Derek. Another chapter in his need to murder women. She opened it and read the first couple paragraphs, but had no desire to throw herself into murder yet. She closed it down also and went to take a quick nap.

The country air had an effect on her that made her restful and sleepy. She crashed on the couch and watched the clouds floating by outside the windows. Shortly she was asleep.

Her dreams filled with the vision of her walking into her husband's studio but not finding him or her friend Betsy whom he was painting a portrait of. She moved through the hallway towards the bedroom. The walls seemed to shift and weave around her. She felt a tremor in her body as she went to the door. It seemed to be pulsating like the beating of a heart. She was afraid to reach for the doorknob, but she was compelled to. She turned the knob, but it just slipped in her hands. Then it grabbed onto her hand and turned itself. The door slowly opened. The room was dark save for a small light from the bathroom off to the side. She forced herself to enter and turned her head toward the bed. The horrific scene of her husband in bed with her best friend and all the blood around them shocked her once again.

Sarah screamed, not in her dream, but from the couch she was on. She sat up quickly and moved the hair from her face. The sweat was pouring from her face and she stood shakily, went to the kitchen and grabbed a towel. She wiped her face and turned on the water in the sink. She grabbed a glass and took a big drink of the cool liquid. She put the glass down and ran her hands under the still running water. She splashed her face with it to wake herself up completely and took deep breaths. She wiped her face again and went back to the living room.

She sat at her desk again and opened the e-mail she had from her boss. A manuscript of a romance novel. Good choice to get her mind off the dream. She had only a couple of those dreams since the night it actually happened, but more than once was too much. She didn't need them out here, so far from where it happened.

She read the chapter. It was a steamy romance novel with plenty of good sex. She blushed at some of the passages between the hero and heroine. It was one of those historical romances with swashbuckling men and swooning women. She had read many of those in her career as editor. Her company had started to handle more of them. They sold well. Women just couldn't get enough of reading about sex.

Sarah finished the manuscript, making her edits here and there. She closed it up and sent it back to Hal or whoever was receiving his mail. She was feeling better. Books always took her to another world, lifting her out of her reality.

She was hungry and went to the kitchen to check the food she had bought earlier. Nothing looked good to her, and she didn't feel like cooking or even nuking anything in the microwave. She went to get her coat again and grabbed the keys.

She got into her car and drove back towards the town. She had seen a restaurant in her journey earlier so she drove there, found it again and parked. Entering the place that was half full, she went to an empty booth and sat. A young waitress bounced up and said, "Welcome to the Halfway House. Would you like some water?"

"Sure, that would be nice."

The girl went off after giving Sarah a menu. She was looking through it as she felt a presence next to her. She looked up into the bright blue eyes of Sheriff Dave Chandler.

*

Chapter 7

Derek awoke early, took a long hot shower, and dressed. Feeling more awake now, he organized his thoughts as to how he would answer any questions the police would ask. He was covered well enough. He had an alibi to satisfy Flint. He went out to his Caddie and drove back to the police precinct. He parked and went to the lobby, again finding the same big cop writing in the big book. Maybe he was an aspiring author, too, Derek mused. The cop saw Derek and quickly picked up his phone.

Fatal Rejection

The officer called Detective Flint who shortly entered the lobby of the precinct and found Derek Harcourt resting on the bench. "Mr. Harcourt, nice of you to come in. I was going to send a couple of my men to go look for you since you didn't tell me where you were staying. Of course, I didn't think it would be relevant to know. Would you please follow me?"

Harcourt stood and followed Flint back to his cubicle. He sat next to the desk. Before Flint could start, Derek spoke. "I figured you'd want to talk to me after I saw the news report about the suspicion of murder by the NY Slasher. Quite a coincidence, I must say," Derek said nonchalantly.

"Yes, it was. I immediately thought of you. What type of car do you drive, Mr. Harcourt?"

"I own a 2010 Cadillac CTS. It's in your parking lot if you'd like to look at it."

"Not necessary. Luckily for you we had a witness to the crime, and I think we can rule you out."

"Oh, how so?"

"The murder was committed in a motel, a cheap one with thin walls. The person registered in the room next to where the crime took place became annoyed when he heard the water running continuously in the crime scene bathroom. Then he heard the room entrance door open and close but the water kept running. He looked out through his window curtains and saw a tall man all in black going down the stairs to the parking lot. The suspect drove out in a Chevy Suburban, not a Cadillac. The water kept running so the man called down to the office and complained. When the desk clerk came up to check, he entered the room and found the victim on the bed, dead."

"Terrible. Any leads on the suspect?"

"None yet, but just to ease my mind, where were you from about 1 a.m. to 2 a.m.?"

"I was in my motel room typing my chapter about the past murder here in your city. Then I sent it off to my editor around 3 a.m. and went to bed. I can e-mail you a copy of the chapter if you'd like. Also, your forensic people can check the time stamp on my files as I save them to the hard drive. It should show I was working on the chapter from about 11 p.m. to 3 a.m. when I sent the e-mail and just before I retired."

"Yes, I'd like a copy of the chapter, just to see how you treated the past incident here in our city. I'm a stickler for accuracy."

"Excellent! I'd like your feedback on it. I also care about details. Now, am I a suspect?"

Fatal Rejection

"I don't think at this point you are, but I may need to talk with you again."

"Well, I had planned to move on to follow my journey if I can leave by tomorrow. Would that be possible?"

"Yes, it's possible. Do you have a card with your cell phone number?"

Harcourt took out his business card and handed it to Flint.

"I don't have much more for you, Mr. Harcourt. Just let me know when you plan on leaving our city," Flint said and handed Derek his card.

"I'll be sure to do that, Detective. And thank you again for the information yesterday."

He smiled, left Flint's cubicle and went out to his car. He stood looking around at all the tall buildings of Buffalo. He thought to himself that maybe someday he would come back to explore. For now he had a plan and didn't want to delay it, and in the next city he wanted less contact with the police.

Detective Flint was watching Derek from the windows of the precinct as he drove away. He turned to Detective Clark, his partner, and said, "Go put someone on Harcourt's motel and have him watched. I'm not trusting coincidences, and the man is a bit creepy. Run a background check on him also. He may be using an alias to write with. Give his publisher out in New York a call and find out."

The detective went off, and Flint turned back to the window to look at the city he grew up in and now protected. He didn't want any more murders.

Derek satisfied himself with Buffalo wings from the restaurant that first started the craze. He wolfed down the nuggets of hot spicy chicken and finished it off with a good pilsner. He left the restaurant after taking a couple pictures of the building for his scrapbook then went back to his motel.

Once in his room he checked his e-mail and found nothing for him, no corrections on his new chapter. Maybe Sarah was busy still getting her new home set up. He was surprised when she moved across the country to live in total seclusion, but he wouldn't expect less from her.

He pulled the business card Flint gave him and e-mailed his chapter. No sense in having Flint annoying him for the file. Better to send it than have Flint come after him for it. He sent the file and closed up his laptop, turned on the TV and found an old movie, "The Boston Strangler." How amusing, Derek thought and sat back to watch.

~~*~~

Fatal Rejection

Detective Clark had no luck tracking down Harcourt's past. It was as if he didn't exist prior to his first book. Clark didn't have much luck getting information from his publisher either. He got a runaround there as no one wanted to admit Harcourt's real name. He would need a court order to make them talk, but without probable cause he'd never get a judge to sign. Flint was annoyed with the lack of information and was more determined than ever to find out who Harcourt was. It was late now and he was worn out, so he told Clark to go home then sat back at his desk and did a Google search on Harcourt. He found very little, and then said the hell with it. He shut everything down and went home.

~~*~~

Early the next morning Derek settled with the motel and left a message for Flint that he was leaving town. He headed towards the freeway that would take him out of Buffalo. He drove down the highway and glanced over to the car rental agency where yesterday he rented the black Chevy Suburban under an assumed name, the car he used when he killed the woman in the motel. He smiled quietly to himself and left Buffalo behind on his way to his next stop, Toledo, Ohio.

Chapter 8

"I hope I'm not interrupting. May I join you?" the sheriff asked.

"If I say no, will you harass me or entrap me in a speed trap?"

"We small town police don't do that. We leave that to the big city cops."

Sarah smiled and sighed. "Sure, have a seat. Did Lois send you?"

"No, I haven't seen her since the grocery store. Why? Is she trying to set you up with me?"

"Well, she has good intentions. I'm vulnerable and alone now, so she thinks I need a man."

"Do you? Not being too personal, I hope."

"I'm getting over my husband's death. My emotions have to heal. One reason I left New York, I got tired of people worrying about my mental health."

"Well, don't worry about me. My mental health is a little stretched right now, too. I just got out of a relationship with a woman I thought I really loved. Five years we lived together, and everything was great. She didn't like the fact I was a cop, but she put up with it. Then one day a month ago, she just left. She took my heart and my life when she flew off to Seattle. She didn't even have the decency to explain, just flew the coop leaving one note saying she was finished. Good bye, Charlie."

"Was she from around here, too?"

"Too? No, she wasn't. I lived here until just before I met her, then I moved to Tacoma, just south of Seattle, to be with her, but I got an offer to be sheriff here. We both moved back out here from Tacoma. I took this job after I left the Tacoma police, and she came with me. Small town living didn't appeal to her. She was a big city girl. So she finally packed it in and left."

"I'm sorry. I guess we're both hurting now. Shall we start our own therapy group?"

The sheriff laughed. "Sure, I know a couple more heartbroken people we can suck in. Small towns aren't exempt from bad relationships."

The waitress came back with the glass of water. She asked, "Are you ready to order? Hi, Sheriff Dave. How are you today?"

Sarah could see the young girl was smitten with the sheriff. She smiled to herself.

"I'm fine, Clara. Are you working hard?" the sheriff answered.

"Oh, yes. I have put in overtime three times this week. The other girls don't like to come in when they should. They should be worried about their jobs. They could lose them if they keep goofing off. But, no, they think I'll do all the work for them. They are so wrong…"

The sheriff held up his hand, and Clara stopped talking. She gathered herself up, realizing she had a customer. "I'm sorry. What would you like to order, ma'am?" she said to Sarah.

"Please call me miss. I'm not old enough for ma'am yet. I'd like the steak and eggs and a coffee."

Clara wrote down the order and went off after giving Dave a big smile.

"She's a little young for you." Sarah giggled.

"I know that. I used to date her mother before Clara was even born. Thanks for making me feel old."

"Sorry, I just wanted to keep you from doing something you might regret."

"Well, I am a grown up and not dumb like some men. You are more my age, but of course, we have our problems so you don't need to worry about me."

"Sorry, but I'm off the market."

"Well, that's a good attitude, I guess," he said just as his belt radio signaled. He answered, and Sarah could hear the conversation over the walkie-talkie.

"Sheriff, this is Mike."

"I know, Mike, you're the only other person with a radio. What is it?"

"Got a call from the state police. They said they think the serial killer may be heading this way. They found a body just south of Gig Harbor. Same M.O. as the rest out in Seattle."

"Well, that's still across all the lakes, not necessarily anywhere near us. Did they say that the killer may be coming our way?"

"No, they just wanted to give us a heads up. Just in case."

"Makes sense. Thanks, Mike. How are things out there?"

"All quiet until the VFW lets out later, but I'll keep it under control."

"If the boys give you any trouble, call me."

"Will do, Sheriff. Over and out."

Dave smiled and clipped the radio back on his belt. "Sorry about that. He's my deputy, young and eager."

"Is this Gag Harbor close?"

"Gig Harbor, and it's quite a ways from us. Lots of roads to go before the killer would waste his time out here."

"I hope so. I didn't move almost three thousand miles to have serial killers in my neighborhood. You'll protect me, won't you?"

"Of course. Besides, if I didn't, Lois would hound me to death. I have to be going. Enjoy your meal. The steak and eggs are great. I eat them at least once a week."

"You don't cook?"

"Oh, I'm a great cook, but every now and then I have to eat out while working."

"A great cook? Are you good with breakfast?"

Fatal Rejection

"I make fantastic pancakes. Too bad you'll never find out."

"I could call for police protection with a problem early in the morning." Sarah smiled.

Dave stood and said, "I'll send Mike to take care of your problem." He smiled, went off and out the front door.

Okay, so she was starting to like him, not in a romantic way, but he was nice. And not bad to look at. About ten minutes later her order came and, she had to admit, the steak and eggs were good. In fact, the best she ever had. She would be back.

It was very quiet in the house. She thought about getting a dog just to keep her company. Maybe tomorrow she'd see if they had a dog pound there and pick out a rescue dog. She never had a dog, so she wondered if they were a lot of work. Not that she had a lot to do. Her edits took very little of her time, so she could have plenty of time to spend working with a dog.

It was late, and she climbed into bed. She lay there thinking about all the changes she had gone through—the move, the people in her life, and a serial killer on the loose. She wasn't worried about the killer. According to the sheriff he was still too far away to worry about. But even in small towns they had their killers. Look at all the "Chainsaw" movies and that "Psycho" movie—small town murders. She had to stop thinking about that or she was guaranteed bad dreams.

She got up, went to the kitchen and opened the cupboard. Inside she had a fifth of bourbon for special occasions. Lack of sleep warranted a special occasion. She poured a healthy portion of the liquid into a glass and took it to the living room. She sat at her desk and stared at the blank screen of her computer. She was just taking a sip of her drink when she heard a loud banging noise outside the window. She almost dropped her drink, but caught herself. She heard it again and stood, picking up a heavy bust of the poet William Wordsworth from her desk. She went to the curtain of the window where the noise came from. She pulled the curtain back slightly and peeked out. She was shocked to see two eyes staring back at her, the eyes of a raccoon.

Damn, she thought. Wild life does make noise, something she didn't have in the city. She opened the curtain wider, scaring the raccoon off, and laughed at the incident. She took a big swig of the bourbon and went to the kitchen for more. She downed the drink and was feeling the effects of it so she went back to bed and figured she'd sleep well now. But she started to have thoughts about Sheriff Dave. She loved her husband, but it had been so long since she had been in bed with a man. The romance novels didn't help much either. They just made it harder to not think about sex.

She finally drifted off. Her sleep was not given to bad dreams, but she did dream about Sheriff Dave.

*

Chapter 9

He was thirty miles from Buffalo, so Derek set the cruise control and relaxed. No cop car flashers in his rear view mirror, no calls on his cell phone from Detective Flint asking him to return. He glanced at the scenery whizzing by on the route around Lake Erie to Toledo. Later, as he approached Toledo, he pulled over and parked on the side of the highway to rest from the long drive. As he sat there he thought back to how this all started, that damn letter from that damn woman, crushing him so severely that he snapped.

Long before his book was finally accepted by a publisher, he had spent a couple years reading and studying serial killers, mostly the NY Slasher, and he often wondered what it was like to take a life. After his book was finally published, he thought about writing a second to keep his success going. He plotted an outline of a story that would satisfy his burning desire for revenge on the woman who hurt him so badly, taking him to depths of his soul that he never dreamed he could ever reach.

The woman, Sarah Keller, was still working at the publishing company in New York, not far from where he lived in his run down piece of crap apartment. He had gone there to scout out the building and finally found her, staying carefully back so she never saw him. He followed her as she went to and from work, and he knew her habits, when and where she ate, who she spent time with at work. He watched her with her husband as they left their new home to go out to eat or to the store. He became obsessed with the woman.

The husband was some kind of artist, a painter, he had heard. He had a studio in their house that he worked from, hardly leaving the dwelling unless with his wife. Derek was sinking deeper into a depression that had to be satisfied. He made a plan for his first kill, the woman and, if need be, her husband. He felt an excitement growing as he plotted the way he would do it. He would wait until one night when she and her husband were relaxing in their home, quietly break in and incapacitate them with the stun guns he had purchased online. Then he would do what he felt like with her, satisfying his base needs. He assembled various tools he would use—rope, knives, duct tape and plastic bags to remove any evidence. Placing everything in a gym bag, he put it in the trunk of his car and looked at his watch. He had a couple hours to kill before he figured the young couple would be relaxing.

After he filled himself with a meal from a local restaurant, he got back into his car and drove out to the quiet subdivision where they lived. He parked near a secluded patch of trees, walking the couple of city blocks to the house. He went to the back of the building and tried to peer into windows to see where they might be. He went to the back door and carefully worked the lock the way he was taught by his cellmate in Iona State Prison back in Michigan when he was serving time for his youthful crime.

The lock yielded. He slowly entered the building with his stun guns in hand and listened. He heard no television playing as he went down the hallway towards where he presumed the bedrooms to be. He saw a light on in one room and went to the door. All he could see through the crack in the door was Sean Keller standing before a canvas, painting a portrait of a woman. The painting must have been just started as there were no discernible features of the face. Derek figured he was painting Sarah. He slowly opened the door and carefully aimed the one stun gun at the man and pulled the trigger. The thin wires flew out and hit the man in his side causing him to yelp when the voltage flowed out. He dropped to the floor.

Derek came around the corner and aimed the second stun gun at the woman he believed to be Sarah. He was shocked to find it wasn't her. He fired the stun gun and incapacitated the woman. He looked around to see if Sarah was in the room, but could find no one else. He called to her, risking exposure, but received no reply.

He stood there in silence examining the situation. He wanted so badly to kill Sarah. This was not as planned. Then he had an idea. If he couldn't kill her physically, he would kill her in a different way.

He carried each body to the master bedroom, undressed them both and placed them on the bed. He then removed his clothing, placed it in the plastic bag and proceeded to stab the woman repeatedly and cut both of Sean's wrists. They both bled out quickly. He was careful not to get splattered by the blood then wiped the knife handle of prints and placed it in Sean's hand, pressing down on the fingers to put his prints on the handle. A perfect murder-suicide.

He packed all his equipment back in the gym bag, dressed again and took a couple of pictures of the scene with his cell phone. He stood thinking that Sarah would think they were lovers and possibly had a romance gone bad. She would be devastated, and her life would crumble. His plan was not perfect and would have some holes, but no one could associate him with this crime. The cops would be so confused by what must have happened that the case could go on forever or be ruled quickly as murder-suicide. He made one last check to be sure he left no evidence then backtracked out, wiping anything he might have touched, and left the house.

There was a knocking on his car window, bringing him out of his thoughts. He was startled to see a big cop standing just back from his driver's door. He rolled the window down. "Yes, officer, did I do something wrong?"

"Are you alright?"

"I'm fine, just resting from a long drive from Buffalo."

"I drove by here twice and didn't see you moving, so I was just checking. Are you sure you're alright?"

"Yes, sir, I am. I'll get back on the highway and proceed to Toledo. Thank you for your concern."

"Okay, watch for cars and drive carefully." The cop went back to the patrol car with flashers going, and then he shut them down.

Crap, Derek thought. The cop probably ran his plates through the LEIN. Now they knew he was heading into town. Any more fatal mistakes like this could be his downfall. He had to be more alert. He started the car and drove away leaving the cop still on the shoulder, probably making a report of Derek's faux pas.

He found a cheap motel next to a restaurant and got a room. He went in to eat at the greasy spoon. After he ordered his food, he took out his Moleskin note book and opened it to a page that had gibberish written on it. He smiled at the crude code he devised to hide his list of women he planned on killing along his journey across the country. He had crossed off his first two kills and read the next on the list, the woman who lived in Toledo, a book agent he found on the Internet. Not a book editor like the last two, but just as evil. He would find her and take her out also.

*

Chapter 10

Sarah was showering the next morning thinking about the dream she had of the sheriff. No sexual activity, but he did rescue her from the attack raccoon. She hated dreams. They usually intruded on her feelings when she got up in the morning, leaving her sometimes mixed up or emotionally drained.

A dog was a better idea than having the sheriff save her from danger or rabid wild animals. Maybe she could find a pit bull and train it to ward off intrusive visitors from her life, too.

Fatal Rejection

She toweled off and stood looking around her bathroom. It was huge, the biggest she'd ever been in. There was a separate shower stall from the bathtub and a nice vinyl covered bench next to it with a radiant warmer above. She could slip out of the shower and relax while being heated as she dried. The sink counter was about six feet wide with two bowls, enough room to put out lots of make-up and accessories to make her look good. But why look good now? No one was going to see her. Not like in New York where she competed against young, good-looking secretaries and co-workers every day at her office. Her co-workers here were raccoons and deer.

She went to her bedroom through the connecting door from the bathroom and to the wide walk-in closet where she studied all the clothing she brought with her. Most of the dresses were too fancy for Brinnon unless they had pageants or fancy balls in town. She selected a sweater and casual slacks to put on, not too fancy or presumptuous, just nice enough to go into town.

She went to the kitchen and pulled out the phone directory. It wasn't very big compared to the five pound New York phone book. She ran through it looking for anything about dogs or dog pounds. She found nothing, so she pulled out her cell phone and called Lois.

"Dear, I was just thinking about you," Lois said when she found out it was Sarah.

Sarah hoped she didn't have any other men for her to meet. "I need to know if there is a dog pound or pet shop around where I could get a dog."

"A dog? Dear, you don't need a dog, you need a man. I heard that you had dinner with Dave last night. Was it good?"

"Lois, I went to get some food. He was in the restaurant and sat with me briefly, no big romantic dinner. Oh, and the steak and eggs are great."

"Aren't they? Best in Washington State. Are you meeting with Dave again?"

"Lois, give it up and just tell me where I can find a dog."

Sarah could hear Lois laughing, then she said, "There is an animal rescue place about five miles south of you. A small building with a big sign out front. They take in strays and give them a place to stay until they get adopted. It's run by Doris and Hank Potter, a nice older couple. They don't have family so they treat their animals as their children."

"Thanks, Lois. I'll give it a try. I'll talk to you later."

Fatal Rejection

"Dave is a cat lover, but I'm sure his cat and your dog could get along," Lois said before Sarah could hang up.

"I'll keep that in mind. Got to go. Thanks Lois," she said and hung up. That woman was going to drive her nuts. She got her purse and keys and went out to the car. It was a sunny morning. She needed that. She turned left on the main road, heading south until she saw the sign, "Happy Pets Sanctuary and Rescue." She pulled into the drive and over to an area of gravel for parking. She went to the entrance of the building. The sign on the door said to just come in. She opened the door and was met by three tiny dogs yipping at her ankles. They made her laugh.

A rotund grey-haired woman came out from a door off the side of the lobby and smiled. "Welcome, young lady. Are you here to adopt a pet?"

"I'm thinking of it. What do you have?" she said.

The woman smiled again and said, "We have just about any kind of animal you could want. I'm sure you're not wanting a python, even though we have one. Are you looking for a cat or dog?"

"I think a dog, something to be a companion and watch dog."

"Dogs make the best companions, but don't tell the cats that. They may be independent but they are

68

great friends. Come with me. I'll take you to our dog kennel." She led Sarah out to a large backroom, apparently an addition to the house. There were many cages, each with a dog bouncing as they came up.

"Take your time, dear. Picking a dog is not something you do quickly. You have to be able to bond with them."

Sarah walked down the row of cages, examining each dog in the clean cages. She could see they were well taken care of. She came around to another row and stopped at one cage. A Terrier with a big chunk of its ear missing sat there quietly. Must have lost the ear in a fight with another animal, she thought. She knelt down, and the dog put its nose up to the cage as Sarah poked her finger through and rubbed his nose. He was enjoying the attention. Sarah asked the woman what his story was.

"He came to us from some people who were moving away. I don't think they treated him very well. He was head shy when we got him."

Sarah looked at the missing chunk of ear and said, "I'll call him Van Gogh after the painter, my husband's favorite. He cut off his ear for a love." She stood and told the woman, "I'll take him."

The woman called to someone named Hank, and an elderly man came in from a side room. "Dear, this is my husband Hank," she told Sarah. To the man she said, "Bring this dog up to the front while I get the adoption papers ready for this woman. Come with me, dear."

They went back up to the lobby, and the woman brought out very cleverly made adoption papers. She scribbled the information as to the time and place of adoption then signed her name and handed the paper to Sarah.

The man came around the counter with the dog on a leash. Sarah knelt again and ruffled the dog's head. He licked her hand, and she laughed.

"Good sign, he likes you," said the man.

"How much do I owe you?" Sarah asked.

"Oh, we work on a donation system here. We couldn't sell our children. Whatever you feel is worth it to help take care of them," the woman said.

Sarah took out her checkbook and made it out. She handed the check to the woman and smiled. "I hope this helps with your cause." She looked down to Van Gogh and said, "Ready to go home with me?"

It was almost as if the dog understood. He bounced a couple times and started for the door. Sarah laughed and said to the couple, "I guess that's a yes." Then she went out.

The woman looked at the check. It was made out for $300. She showed it to the man and smiled. "Such a kind woman."

Sarah was amazed that the dog sat so quietly on the front seat next to her. She half expected the dog to put its head out the window, then she realized the window was closed. She pushed the button to lower the window, just a bit so the dog couldn't jump out. Van Gogh saw the window open and went right for it, putting his head out and enjoying the wind on his face.

Sarah laughed and wondered why dogs liked to do that. She'd have to do a Google search for the answer. She arrived back home and took the dog's leash before opening the car door. She didn't want him to go running off into the woods next to her house. She wanted the dog to get to know her first. She led the dog to the side door going into the utility room and then into the kitchen. She realized she had no dog food, so she checked what she had in her refrigerator. Nothing good for dogs.

"Oh, well, I'll just have to take a trip into town again. We'll get a chance to show you off. How's that?"

The dog was bouncing again. Sarah got her purse and keys and led the dog out to the car. She opened the door. The dog went right for the passenger seat and sat. "At least I don't have to train you in car etiquette."

She went back to the Brinnon General Store and left the dog in the car. They probably didn't like dogs in the store. She wandered the aisles and found the pet section. She gathered food and other supplies then paid. She was on her way to the car when she saw that the sheriff's car was blocking her car. Dave got out and came to her.

"Did I break a law?" she asked.

"I'll think of something to arrest you for. I see you have a dog now. Is this your replacement for a man?" he said with a laugh.

"Yes, at least he obeys and can sleep on the floor. Now if you'll release me, I have to feed my starving puppy."

"Take care and enjoy your new companion." He went back to his car and drove away.

Sarah looked at the dog sitting in her seat watching her as she put the food into the back. "This town is so small it's hard to avoid people. Let's go home and hide."

*

Chapter 11

Doris Cauley smiled at the TV show she was watching as she typed away on her laptop, setting up submissions for the couple of writers she represented. She had been a book agent for just under a year, having been let go from the publishing company. She had worked there for over six years as a book editor. Damn cutbacks and a sluggish economy. The next best thing to do was become an agent, and the few authors she edited for signed up with her.

She lifted the drinking glass that she had filled half up with vodka, her drink of choice lately. She took a sip and shivered. She didn't like the liquid but it made her feel better about herself. Okay, that was a cop out, but it helped the situation since her life was in the toilet now. She had a good rapport with various book publishers, so she was able to be an efficient agent, placing various writers with the companies that would make them famous. Or so they hoped. She knew it was a crapshoot out there and with the e-book revolution, traditional publishers were mostly taking on celebrities and well established authors.

She took a big swig of the drink and sat back in her chair. She stared at the screen of her laptop and wished something in her life would change. She would regret that wish.

Fatal Rejection

Derek approached the house that his next victim occupied and stood studying the property. It was a typical house in the suburbs of Toledo, large lawn and lots of trees which would help in his quest to enter the house unseen. He went around back and checked out the number of windows and doors then made his way to what he presumed was the door to the garage. He was right. He was going to work the lock on the door, but was surprised to find it unlocked. How convenient. He stepped into the dark, smelly garage and nearly tripped on a tool box just inside.

He found the door that he figured went into the kitchen and stood listening. He had done a day's worth of spying on the house already before he felt safe enough to enter. Doris was divorced, no children and self-employed as a book agent. Derek cringed at the word, thinking back to all the agents he was shot down by for his first book. The taste in his mouth was bitter.

He heard nothing at the door and slowly turned the knob. It gave and the door opened. He carefully peeked around the corner and saw no one in the large kitchen. It was well stocked with all types of supplies, pots and pans all neatly hung above the island in the center of the room. On that island he saw a large carving knife in a rack, much nicer than the one he brought with him, so he took it.

Bob Moats

Doris made out well in the divorce. She had a real nice layout of a home, well decorated. The ex was probably living in some cheap motel. He slowly walked down the long hallway to a room that he could hear voices coming from. Not real people talking but voices from a television. You could always tell. It had an odd sound to it, canned and stiff. He got to the door and could see Doris sitting in a chair with her back to him, watching the TV and sipping from a glass.

He carefully opened the door just as he was startled by a tiny yipping coming from around his feet. It was a Chihuahua making enough noise to wake the dead. Doris spun around and dropped her glass at the sight of a man standing in her doorway. She screamed and lunged towards a large vase on her desk, tossing it at Derek. He ducked and fired the stun gun he was holding, hitting her in the stomach. She shook violently as the voltage coursed through her, then she dropped to the floor. Derek reached down and managed to grab the dog by the collar as it squirmed and barked, then flung it into a closet of the room. Just before he could get rid the dog, it bit him on his hand and drew blood.

"Damn," he cursed. He would have to clean up his blood now. No sense in leaving his DNA around the place. He pulled on a new rubber glove, putting the bloodied one in his bag.

Fatal Rejection

He went to Doris, pulled her up from the floor and sat her in the desk chair. He proceeded to fasten her wrists and legs to the chair with zip ties and then duct taped her mouth. He picked up a crystal decanter that was sitting on the desk, smelled the contents and recognized the liquid. He carefully poured some of the vodka into his mouth, being careful not to touch the decanter edge with his lips. The liquid burned on its way down. It tasted good to him.

"Good vodka, Doris. Not the cheap kind, probably Stolichnaya vodka, 100 proof at $28 dollars a bottle. Too bad you hid it in an unmarked decanter. No way to impress your guests," he said with a laugh.

He turned the chair to face her desk and laptop. He shut off the television. He hated the garbage they ran on it. He went over to the vase she threw at him and picked it up from the floor. There was still a good amount of water in it. He removed the flowers and spilled the rest of the water on Doris' head.

She slowly came around and looked at him with bleary eyes. Then she realized her predicament and wanted to scream but the duct tape held it back. She went wide eyed and panicky. Derek slapped her and calmly said to relax.

She knew the gravity of her situation, not good. She quieted down and waited to see what her attacker had in his evil head. Derek walked around behind her and moved up close, caressing her earlobes. She started to struggle again so Derek slapped her on the back of her head.

"Damn it, stop struggling. It won't make it any easier," he said, and she went still. He came around the front of the desk and started to undress, carefully placing his clothing in the plastic bag he carried. He turned to her and gave her an evil smile. "Doris, you should have changed professions to something less dangerous, like a bomb squad tech. But a book agent, not smart."

He walked around behind Doris and picked up the big carving knife he took from the kitchen. "Watch your computer and all the crap you put on it to sell the dreams of writers. Or better yet, to crush their dreams with a slush pile rejection. A fatal rejection on your part. But this will only hurt for a short time."

He pulled her head back and slit her throat with the knife, blood spraying from her cut arteries. The blood covered the computer and desk. Derek held his hand in the stream and then wiped it on his chest and arms. He laughed and then went around the front to watch her die.

When she had finally expired, Derek went to the bathroom and showered, leaving the water running to wash away all trace. He toweled off using a towel he had brought with him and then dressed. He took a couple pictures of the scene and carefully checked to see that he left no evidence of his being there. Besides, who would suspect him?

He left the house and walked the couple blocks to his car, carefully parked in an area where the police wouldn't investigate. He got in after placing his bag in the trunk and started the car, driving away.

He got back to his motel, opened up his laptop and wrote his next chapter, the murder of a woman in Toledo. He didn't mention her profession which might make Sarah wonder why his character was killing people in the book business. No sense giving away too many details before he had to deal with her. He had big plans for the death of Sarah Keller.

*

Chapter 12

Van Gogh finished wolfing down the food Sarah put down for him and went out to where Sarah was sitting at her desk working. He sat looking up at her. She stopped and petted his head.

"Good boy, Van Gogh," she said, wanting to repeat his name enough to get him used to it. She never asked if he came to the dog sanctuary with a name. She figured he was starting over also. They both were.

She was working on her free-lance edits for the couple chapters that came in while she was gone. Harcourt hadn't sent one today, thankfully. Van Gogh lay down at her feet and made a huffing noise, then closed his eyes. She looked at the dog and had a good feeling about this.

She worked for about an hour then stretched. She got up, causing the dog to jump. He stood watching her as she went towards the vestibule and put her coat on again. Then the dog started jumping around by the door. He seemed to know they were going out.

"You are one smart dog, Van Gogh. Shall we take a walk?" She got the new extendable leash device that she had bought at the store. It could give the dog more line to run but she could pull him back with the push of a button. She hooked it to his collar then opened the door. The dog just about took her arm off running out. She held on tightly and then slowly let out more line to give him a chance to smell around the grounds.

As she stood in the yard, she heard a car pulling into the drive. She and the dog went around the house to see which pest was coming to bother her this time. The car wasn't familiar. It stopped by her car and a girl in her late teens got out and came to her.

"Mrs. Keller?" the young girl asked.

Fatal Rejection

"I am. May I help you?"

"I really hope I'm not intruding. I heard you were an editor for a publishing company."

"Yes, I am," she said, thinking that this girl was probably a writer wanting to get her story read. She had that happen a lot of times. There were just too many people out there who thought they could write.

"If I'm not being presumptuous, I have a manuscript that I wonder if you could read and give me an honest opinion, if I have any talent for writing."

There it was. She hoped there weren't more writers hiding in the woods. "Well, I'm a busy person with my edits, but..." She could see this young girl was looking hopeful. She hated to tell the girl no. It might hurt her. She could be diplomatic about turning her down, but, what the hell, it wasn't like she had a busy social life. "I can take a look, but you have to promise not to tell anyone or I'll be having to read everyone's stories."

"Oh, I won't say a word. I have let my mom read it and she thinks it's good, but she's my mom. She has to say that."

"Moms are like that. Do you have your manuscript?"

Bob Moats

"Yes, wait…" she said and ran to her car, took out a thick manila envelope and brought it back. "Here. It's only a short story, but it's complete. I hope you'll be honest with me. I know some people who write, and they are terrible. It's hard to say they are, so they go on thinking they can write."

"Yes, I saw it every day in the submissions I used to get from hopeful writers. It is hard to tell them their work is trash, but if I didn't, they'd go on believing they could write when they should be doing something else."

"Exactly. I always do well in my English class. My stories have gotten some praise by my teachers, but you are a professional in the business. You really know what is good."

"Well, I'm not always right. Every editor has his own opinion as to what is worth publishing. Sometimes we reject a book that some other company picks up and makes a success out of it. Look at J.K. Rowling. Her Harry Potter books were turned down by twelve publishers before she became famous. She's the bestselling author in the world now."

"Yes, I'll bet those other publishers are kicking themselves."

"I'm sure they are. I'll give this a look and let you know. By the way, who are you?"

Fatal Rejection

"Oh, I'm sorry, I should have introduced myself. My name is Denise Cole. I live in town and my phone number is on the first page."

"Great, Denise. Give me a few days, but please be patient. And don't be too upset with my honesty."

"I won't, thanks."

"By the way, how'd you know I was out here?"

"My aunt told me, Lois Carter. She says she knows you. Well, I'll let you get back to what you were doing. Nice dog," she said looking at Van Gogh, who was busy sniffing at the girl's feet.

"Yes, he's new to me. I just got him. I'll call when I'm finished reading. As I said, give me a couple days."

"Thank you," Denise said and went back to her car.

Sarah watched the girl drive off. She looked at Van Gogh and said, "Lois is sending her family to bug me now. I hope this story is good, or I'll have Lois at my door with an ax. Shall we go back in, if you're finished with your business out here?"

Bob Moats

They went back into the house, and Sarah let the dog loose. He ran off into another room. Sarah went to the kitchen to make some coffee.

She was sitting comfortably on the couch with the manuscript Denise gave her. She had nothing better to do, so she read. About an hour later, she had read it twice. There were errors in the grammar and phrasing, but Sarah enjoyed the story. It was very good. She took it to her desk, got out her red pencil and made some comments and changes, then put it back in the envelope. She'd call Denise later to keep the poor girl from worrying and tell her to come back out tomorrow. It was starting to get late and she hadn't eaten anything all day. She always forgot to eat when she was working. It was one way she kept so slim. She went to the kitchen followed by the dog who came out of hiding from somewhere in the house.

"Are you always going to show up when I go in the kitchen, Van Gogh?" She laughed.

The dog wagged his tail and sat, twisting his head from one side to the other. She laughed at his cute pose and opened the refrigerator. She pulled out the cold cuts she bought the same time she got the dog food and took them to the counter. She was going to have her ham sandwich finally.

The dog was fed again and Sarah was happy with her sandwich. It wasn't New York deli style, but it tasted as good. She sat at her computer again to finally reply to Connie's e-mail. She didn't want Connie worrying about her if she took too long to reply.

"Connie, hope all is well back in the office. I'm getting my manuscripts regular and sending them back. So far Hal hasn't bitched too much. It's nice being away from his constant intrusions, coming into my office a dozen times a day asking if I'm finished. I'm hopeful for your romance with the investment broker. I have a cute sheriff chasing me out here. No details yet. I'm not real interested in him, but it's good to know I'm still desirable. Yes, you really need to come out here, it's so peaceful and quiet, but you'd probably hate it. There are no clubs to go to other than a VFW hall. I do have a cell phone, you know, same number I had when I was in New York, so you can call me if you feel like it. Take care, Sarah."

She hit the send button and sat back. Van Gogh came up and put his head on her lap. He was just tall enough to put it there. She rubbed his head and thought about what she was going to do with the rest of her life. Sean was gone now. She had to eventually face the fact. She knew she liked having a man around, but was she ready to invest the time into another romance? Dave was actually a good catch, but he was a cop. What if she he got romantic with him and he was in a shootout and got killed? Not a good prospect for a relationship. If he was a salesman or a store manager…but she figured he'd never go for that. She decided to play it by ear and see what would come tomorrow.

She moved Van Gogh away and reached to her desk phone. Taking the number from Denise's manuscript, she called her. Denise was surprised that Sarah called so soon.

"I just want to say you are very good at telling a story. You're still rough with the grammar and structure, but that is why there are editors out there. Come by tomorrow and we'll go over your story. Is that good for you?"

She could hear the girl's excitement in her voice. "Oh, yes, I can be there, what time?"

"How about one in the afternoon?"

"I'll be there. I'm so excited." They said their good-byes and hung up.

Sarah looked at Van Gogh and said, "I just made her day."

*

Chapter 13

Detective Healy stood by the door staring at the bound body of the woman in the crime scene as the ME was making his examinations. It brought back some old memories that he had tried to forget, but this was just dredging up bad thoughts.

Detective Ross, Healy's much younger partner, came up and said, "Forensics says the perp took a shower then left the water running, probably to be sure to wash away any evidence. I've seen some grisly murders but this is just mean. Making her sit at her desk and slice open her throat, just mean."

"If I didn't know better, I'd say either we have the return of a long forgotten killer or a copycat." Healy spoke softly. "I'd venture it's a copycat."

"What? You've seen this before?"

"About fifteen years ago, NY Slasher as he was called back then. Spread his hateful murders across the United States killing over 30 women, then he just vanished. He hit Toledo and murdered two women before he moved on. This has the same M.O., but, as you said, it has a bit of meanness to it. Did you finish questioning the cleaning woman?"

"Yep. Says she arrived this morning, looked for Cauley and found her in here. She says she touched nothing, just ran for the phone to call 911. She's a bit upset, so I'll finish questioning her in a while. Luckily she speaks English well enough to understand her. She's from Mexico."

"If this guy was as careful as the NY Slasher, we won't get much evidence. So far they got zip here. Either he'll hit one more woman or be on the move. But we do have to investigate, so I'm sure we'll have any number of suspects that could have wanted this woman dead. Are you ready to go play detective?" Healy smiled at the younger man.

~~*~~

Derek had a full breakfast, sat back in the booth feeling satisfied and then looked at his notebook again. He crossed off his latest kill and then smiled at his next destination, Detroit, the hometown he was so glad to be out of and the evil he left there. He had no idea if his old man was still alive. He lost touch after he split out at age eighteen. After he got out of prison, he never went back to the city, making New York his new home. But he looked forward to seeing if the fucker was still alive. He had a taste of blood, and it wouldn't bother him to murder the bastard, too.

Fatal Rejection

He paid the bill for the food. It was passable, but not the best he'd had. He went back to his motel and packed. He had no intention of any further murders in Toledo. He had to keep to his schedule and had a long way to go across the country. Detroit was only a little over an hour from Toledo, so he could hit the old homestead and then be on his way out. He had just one thing to do, and he hoped he wouldn't be disappointed.

The city hadn't changed much since he last ran the streets of Detroit although a lot more boarded up businesses and burned out houses gave his old neighborhood an eerie sense of abandonment. He pulled down the street he grew up on and found the house he hated. It was still standing amongst many vacant houses, boarded or just left unattended. He drove slowly by and watched carefully for any sign that the old bastard might still be there. He saw the porch chair where his father had sat most of the day and could see the alcohol bottles standing or lying around the porch. That told him maybe the man was still alive.

He drove around to the back alley that ran behind the open garage. He found the family car that never worked right inside. He parked his car and looked around. He could see no one outside. It was as deserted as the front street. He got out from the car and walked around the garage to the small backyard where he used to spend a lot of time while his parents would fight and his father would frequently beat up his mother. He didn't blame her for taking her own life, but she should have taken his, too. Now he would settle the score.

Hc reached the back door and looked around. No one was out or watching, so he banged on the door. He heard a shuffling noise then a voice yelled out, "Who the fuck is it?"

He knew the voice. It was him. Derek brought up his foot and smashed through the door, causing it to crash open. There stood the old man, looking shocked. Derek entered and came up to him, hate raging inside.

"You just had to stay alive all these years, you bastard. You could have committed suicide like you drove my mother to. Well, I guess it's good for me. I have a score to settle with you."

The old man froze at the sight of a son he chased away so many years ago. Derek came up and grabbed the man by the throat then pushed him into a kitchen chair. The man was not strong enough to resist. Booze had taken away his strength and his will to fight. Derek pulled a zip tie from his pocket and tied the man's wrists to the chair. He didn't bother with the legs. The man had no power in them to do any harm.

Derek pulled up a chair backwards and straddled it. "Well, old man, this is nice, now isn't it? I've got your attention and you can't fight me like you did my mother. Remember her? The woman you made a punching bag out of, you son of a bitch. I'm going to enjoy killing you. I'm going to be creative about it, too."

Derek thought better about tying the man's legs to the chair. He didn't want him to be running from what he planned to do. Derek stood and pulled the chair to the living room, placing his father in the center of the room full of trash and clothing. The old man never cleaned the house. That would help accelerate the flames he had planned on starting. Derek found as many of the alcohol bottles as he could and poured the contents around the room on all the papers and assorted trash.

Amazingly the old man never said a word all the time Derek was in the house. This bothered Derek, but he had a job to do. He stood back and struck a match from the matchbox he carried. He dropped the matchstick into the tallest pile of filth and watched it start to flame. Derek watched the old man just sit there, still not saying a word. Then, as the flames were growing, the old man looked Derek in the eyes and said, "Fuck you."

Derek smiled and said, "That's the spirit, you old bastard. Now go to hell." He turned and went out the back door. He could hear the old man howling with pain from the flames. Music to Derek's ears. He got back into his car and drove off, turning up the street as he saw the house going up fast. All the ancient wood and trash made it a funeral pyre for the man he hated all these years. The house was engulfed in flames, all flickering, and he saw the porch where his mother hung herself crash to the ground. He smiled as he watched the place go up and disappear from his life. He drove on, leaving it finally all behind.

Derek was heading out I-94 freeway on his way to Chicago. His next victim awaited there.

*

Chapter 14

Van Gogh rolled over in the bed next to Sarah. She was going to tell the dog to get down last night when he jumped up, but he plopped down next to her and was so warm and comforting, she gave in. It was so long since she had anyone share her bed. Actually, not since Sean. Even if he was a dog, it gave her a good feeling with the body next to her. Of course, she probably was setting a bad example for the mutt, but she'd let this go.

Her bedside alarm went off even though she was already awake. She reached over and shut it off. Van Gogh had shot off the bed when the alarm rang, which surprised Sarah. Maybe some kind of conditioning he went through, she thought. She went to the bathroom through the connecting door. It was nice that the man who built the house put the bathroom between the two bedrooms, and each one had a connecting door to it. The other bedroom was still filled with unpacked boxes that she hoped would just go away. She knew they wouldn't, so she kept the door closed.

She showered and stepped out to see Van Gogh sitting in the middle of the room, staring at her. "Hey, are you some kind of peeping Tom? I don't like to be watched while I shower, so get!" Van Gogh huffed and went back out the door to the bedroom. Sarah thought that was so funny, she started to laugh. She dried off and went back to the bedroom to get dressed. The dog was nowhere to be seen. Probably hurt his feelings by chasing him out of the bathroom, she thought.

She went to the kitchen and found the dog hot on her heels. "You are one strange animal, Van Gogh." He made a small yip and wagged his tail. "Yes, strange indeed." She pulled out the box of dry dog food and poured it in his new bowl. He went for it as soon as she set it down. "You have a good appetite at least."

She made a half-assed breakfast of runny eggs and burnt toast. She never could master the toaster. It always came out too burnt or not toasted enough. She sat at the snack bar between the living area and the kitchen and forced herself to eat. Van Gogh was munching loudly on the kibble she poured for him. She thought about giving the dog the rest of her eggs, but she couldn't be that cruel.

She cleaned the plates and went to her computer to see what torture was waiting for her. She actually had enough money in her bank account to live well for a very long time. Sean's life insurance policy paid well, and since he was murdered, it came in as double indemnity. She wasn't exactly rich, but she was well off. Not the way she wanted to receive the money, but it made life nice, especially if she ever decided to chuck her editing job. But then what would she do? Take up Bingo or start knitting? Maybe she'd get into real estate and give Lois a run for her money.

The computer finally booted up, and she checked the e-mail. She had three from her publisher and one from creepy writer. It was early enough to put up with murder so she edited his first. His storyline was odd. It was mostly about each murder the killer was committing. There was not much of a plot, just the murders of women. They really had no connection to each other, which was usually what serial killers went for. Derek never mentioned how the killer knew the women or why they had to die. She felt there was something missing and maybe that something would eventually come up to put it all in perspective. She hoped it would or she would really hate this book. She finished it and sent off the chapter.

Fatal Rejection

She opened the next three manuscripts. Each had a romantic plot. She needed that after the grisly murder scene.

Van Gogh was barking at the window, and Sarah got up to see what he was carrying on about. She looked out and saw two deer walking through the yard by the fence at the cliff. "Van Gogh, you better not disturb any deer while you live here. That's a no-no," she said harshly, then pointed and wagged her finger at the dog. He flinched his head. She remembered the woman said he was head shy when they got him. Maybe a finger wagging scared him. She knelt, put her hands on each side of his head, and said softly, "Don't worry, puppy. I'll never hurt you." She rubbed the side of her face on his nose, and his tail started wagging again. "Okay, now just leave the deer alone. Deal?"

She worked on the chapters until she heard a car. She looked at the clock. It was one. She remembered that Denise was supposed to come out. She went to the front door as Denise was walking up to the house.

"Well, I like it when someone is punctual. Come on in."

Denise stopped at the steps, and then Sarah saw Lois getting out of the car also. "My aunt takes way too long getting out of a car. I'm sorry, but she insisted on coming along. I hope you don't mind."

94

Bob Moats

"No, quite alright." Sarah wanted to scream but held on and waited for the woman to get to her door. "Lois, welcome. Come in." Sarah visualized slamming the door in her face, knocking her back down the steps and crashing into a heap of arms and legs.

Lois thanked her and came in. Sarah led them to the living room and asked Denise to sit on the couch. Lois was standing by the end of the couch, looking at Van Gogh standing in front of her. The dog lowered his head and actually walked backwards from Lois, then ran away. Sarah thought that was odd and wanted to laugh, but she didn't.

"Strange, I thought dogs liked me. Is he a rescued dog?" Lois said, as she sat.

"Yes, from the place you sent me to. He's still getting used to the house, and you are the first visitors."

"Ah, probably frightened him. Now I understand that you want to publish my niece's writing."

"No, Lois. I told her I liked her work and wanted to go over some corrections in her story. She's a very good writer, but her grammar needs work." She went to the desk and picked up the manuscript, bringing it to Denise. "I'll go over this with you and then you can take it home and correct it. Do you have more stories?"

Fatal Rejection

"I have a stack of them," she said hopefully.

"Okay, bring me a few of them, and we'll see what we can do. I'm not going to say you will get published, but there are ways to self-publish as an e-book. I'll help you with that if you'd like."

"Oh, yeah. That would be great."

"Okay, let's go over this," she said and opened the manuscript to page one. Lois sat quietly listening to them. Sarah thought that was the longest Lois was ever quiet around her.

Sarah saw Van Gogh peek around the corner of the desk where he was hiding. She smiled at the dog, and he went back to lie down.

They went over the changes and Denise was happy. They finished up about an hour and a half later and Sarah announced they were done.

"Take this home and make some corrections that I suggested. It's your story. I just wanted to help you make it better. Please understand that."

They all got up and went to the front door. "Thanks, Sarah. I appreciate it," Denise said and went out.

"I appreciate it also. My niece has been writing since she was old enough to hold a pen. Her mother bought her a computer last year, and she's used that to write her stories."

"Well, she has talent, no doubt. Writing is not an easy occupation to succeed in. I'll help her as much as I can."

"Thanks again," Lois finished and went to the car. Sarah watched them drive off and looked down just inside the door to see Van Gogh standing watching them also.

"What was your problem? I know I'm not real fond of Lois, but you were just plain frightened of her," she said as the dog shook his head and yawned. "Oh, now I bore you? I may just take you back to the farm." She closed the front door and went back to her desk.

She worked on her last chapter and sent it to New York. She sat back just as her phone rang. She answered, "Hello?"

"Sarah, Lois here again. I'm sorry but I forgot to mention that I'm throwing a welcome to Brinnon party in your honor at the VFW hall this Friday night. Now, you can't say no. I've already got the hall and you don't want to disappoint anyone. I'll call again with the details tomorrow. You'll have a great time meeting everyone. Talk later," she said and hung up.

Sarah wanted to scream, but held it back. She looked at Van Gogh lying on the floor with his head down but looking up at her. "How many years in prison would I get if I murdered her?"

His tail started to thump on the floor, and she smiled.

*

Chapter 15

The drive from Detroit to Chicago runs about six hours if a person takes their time. Derek did. He was taking the opportunity to review in his mind the look on his father's face as the flames licked around him. The fire probably would have melted the plastic zip ties from his wrists and feet, so it would look like the old man died in an unexplained house fire. Old house, the man smoked, probably lit it himself after spilling his booze. He stopped thinking about the past and concentrated on the future.

Lindsey Warick, an editor with a prestigious Chicago publishing company, was the next name on his list. He had researched her online and gathered as much as he could about the location of her house.

Bob Moats

The Internet gave out way too much information if a person knew where to look. A successful criminal would be able to find out anything about his victim.

He had always wanted to spend some quality time in Chicago, so he decided to splurge on a first class hotel and went to the Renaissance Blackstone Hotel on Michigan Avenue. He went to the front desk and produced his driver's license, the one that said he was Eugene Petrovskia, the one he carried and carefully renewed ever since before he started using Derek Harcourt for his books. It came in handy when he wanted anonymity.

His room was extravagant, but he could afford it. He set his laptop on the writing desk and opened it up, hooked to the Wi-Fi and checked his mail. He had a reply from Sarah about his last chapter. He read the corrections and smiled. He didn't really care about it. He was playing with her. He shut down that e-mail, and read the other e-mails he received. One came from a person he had befriended online, Max Forbish. They had established a rapport since Max said he was interested in becoming a writer. Derek read Max's e-mail and then replied to him. He explained that he was on a tour across the country to research the NY Slasher's journey of terror. He didn't want to spend too much time answering his fan's letter, but was polite.

He sent out all his replies and closed up the laptop. It was getting close to dinner time, so he went

Fatal Rejection

down to the hotel's restaurant to have a first class meal. Better than the crap he forced himself to eat along the way. He dined alone, although he knew he could pick up a high class escort through the concierge. He didn't need any extra baggage.

He finished his dinner, went back up to his suite, opened up the laptop again and did some more research on Lindsey Warick. He wanted to know all about her. She was a graduate of Radcliffe, the women's liberal arts college, and continued her schooling at Scripps College for women. She was annoyingly educated, Derek thought. He himself was never schooled in formal education and quit before he graduated high school, so persons with a higher education usually pissed him off. He was a graduate of the school of hard knocks, as he often said about his education.

Derek found a resume on her website. She must have been looking for another company to work for. He wondered if her bosses knew. Derek closed down the laptop after he read as much as he could find. He normally wouldn't bother learning too much about one of his victims other than the basics. He usually would learn where they lived and any habits they might have, hobbies, family and activities, but nothing personal about them. This woman was probably the most educated of all his victims, which fascinated him.

He stood, went to the room phone and called down to the concierge. "Yes, this is room 241. Any chance I could get a special massage tonight?" He knew the term was a subtle code for a high class hooker. He smiled at the reply and hung up. Derek decided he was really going to enjoy his stay at this hotel.

~~*~~

Early the next morning Lindsey Warick went to her desk in the back part of her home, sat at the computer all warmed up and ready for her to work. She convinced her boss to let her work at home since she lived twenty-two miles from the publishing company at which she was employed. Cost of gas was her reasoning, although her boss told her she should move closer. She won the argument and was editing out of her home. She thanked the Internet for this, and wondered how people managed before computers. Of course, gas was a lot cheaper then.

~~*~~

Derek drove three times through the neighborhood, studying the house. This might be a little more difficult, he thought. The house was in a row of homes all close to each other, no cover to slip into the building without being seen. There was no alley or back way in. All the yards were backed up to the backyards of the homes behind them. He would have to slip into someone's property to get to his goal. He decided it would be better under cover of darkness, so he drove away to wait for night to fall.

Derek drove up Lakeshore Drive to unwind as he contemplated his attack on Warick's home. He was distracted enough to run a stop sign and found himself being pursued by a cop.

"Shit, I just keep screwing up," he screamed as he pulled over to the shoulder. The cop car whizzed by him and kept going. "Damn, lucky that time. I had better pay attention or just stay in my hotel until it's time to strike. I don't need this crap."

He went back to his hotel and rested in his room, reading the new e-mails that had come in. One was from his new friend Max. He read the mail and chuckled at Max's attempt to get information out of him about his trip. Derek replied that he was in Chicago and heading for Seattle to see his book editor. He apologized for lack of any further facts. He wanted to keep it to himself as to what he was up to. He sent the e-mail and went to the restaurant for dinner.

Around 10 p.m. he drove out of the hotel parking area and back to Warick's home. He parked down the block in a cul-de-sac and made his way in the darkness to Warick's house. Luckily there weren't many street lights on the block, which was strange for a neighborhood of well-to-do residents. He found her house, slipped between the buildings and around the back. It was dark and there were no lights, thankfully for him, he thought.

He tried the back door. It was locked, of course. This woman was intelligent and careful. He worked the tumblers and got the lock to give. He turned the handle and opened the door slowly, waiting for any alarms. He hadn't read in her online biography that she owned a dog, so he hoped she hadn't picked one up since. He stepped into a laundry room and quietly closed the door behind him.

He entered the kitchen with the stun gun in hand and listened. No sounds other than music came from elsewhere in the house. He followed the music down a long hallway and up to a door at the end. He listened and heard nothing but music, no voices or chatter from a late night guest. The door was partially open, and he peeked around the doorframe and saw Lindsey Warick at her desk typing on her computer keyboard and enjoying the classical music that Derek couldn't stand.

He pushed the door open and came up behind her. She was oblivious to his presence until she looked up and saw his reflection in the glass of a window in front of her. She screamed as he grabbed her by the throat and fired the stun gun close into her side. She shook and then went lifeless.

He spun her chair around and stood looking at her. She seemed a bit too lifeless. He checked her pulse at both her wrist and neck and felt nothing. He put his ear close to her nostrils and heard no breathing. He couldn't believe what just happened.

He tasered her to death.

*

Chapter 16

Sarah slept in, then went through her morning routine and actually made a decent breakfast. The eggs were solid and the toast was medium brown. "I'm proud of myself, Van Gogh. I actually made a proper breakfast."

The dog wagged his tail, and she poured his food in his bowl. While he was noisily chomping on the dry chunks of kibble, she went to her desk, started her computer and checked her e-mail. Nothing yet, thankfully. As she sat back, thinking about what she was going to do today, an e-mail popped up on her screen. It was from Derek. "Damn, couldn't even give me a little time to wake up."

She opened the message and read. She was still confused as to the goal of the killer. "What does your serial killer character have in mind, Derek? Inquiring editors want to know."

Van Gogh was sitting next to her chair, and she was startled when she looked down. "Damn dog, you are a quiet one. Are you full now? I hope you don't need to go outside."

The dog started to bounce and then went to the sliding glass door between the floor-to-ceiling windows. He was wagging his tail and panting. "I really do believe you can understand me. Was a teacher your last owner?" She got up and went to the door, checking outside to be sure there were no deer in the back.

"Okay, mutt, I'm going to trust you to go do your business without me and my leash. If you run off and get lost, that's too bad. I'm no scout and probably would get lost myself. Now behave and leave the animals alone." She opened the door and Van Gogh shot out. He stopped about ten feet from the door and turned back to her, waiting. "I said you are on your own, now go poop. I'll pick it up later."

The dog ran off and right out of sight. Sarah thought, "Great, I spend $300 on a dog and he runs off to someone else's home." She closed the door and went back to her desk. She was concerned about the dog, but not much she could do. She couldn't run after him, so she waited.

She was working on Derek's story when she heard a barking outside the door. She looked up, and there was Van Gogh. She went to let him in and said, "I hope you shit in the woods with the bears."

Van Gogh barked at her in response and went to her desk and sat. She went to sit back down again just as her phone rang. She really needed caller ID. When she answered it was Lois.

"Good morning, dear, or it's almost noon, so good afternoon. I just wanted to call and give you the information about your coming out party," Lois said happily. Sarah just felt dread. "Tomorrow night at precisely seven o'clock you are to come to the VFW hall and into the banquet room they have. I've got a number of important people coming that you should know, council people and the mayor. He has to meet you." No, he doesn't, Sarah thought. "Of course, Sheriff Dave will be there." Oh goodie, Sarah said quietly. "What was that dear?"

"Nothing, I just said good. I'll be there. It's casual isn't it, no fancy dresses?"

Bob Moats

"Only if you want to impress a few good men I invited." Damn, Sarah almost said out loud. "So I expect you to be there, right?" Lois said firmly.

"Sure, it will be nice to meet these people." Yeah, like meeting your death squad, she thought.

"Fine, then I'll see you tomorrow night, seven sharp. Don't be late. I only have the room until nine," she said and hung up.

Sarah looked at Van Gogh and said, "Not bad, only two hours of torture. I may bring you to keep the men away from me. Be sure to brush and sharpen your teeth."

Van Gogh lowered his head and slipped away. "Coward!" Sarah yelled after the dog.

She went back to editing Derek's chapter and sent it back. Most of the day was wasted, so she got up and put her coat on. The dog was standing by the door. She put his leash on, and they went out to the car. She drove into town and to the grocery store. She left the dog in the car and went in. She scouted around until she found what she needed, chocolate. She bought fudge bars and cream filled Ho-Hos along with a big bag of chocolate covered donuts. She was going to commit suicide with chocolate.

She paid and left the store, finding no sheriff or Lois blocking her way. She was giving some thought to moving back to New York, but it really wasn't all that bad here. She stood by her car listening to the noises around her. It sounded a bit more city. Cars driving by and businesses doing their business. Around her house the biggest sound was the water from the canal splashing on the shore.

She got back in, and Van Gogh went for the bags. Sarah reached over and pulled them closed. "Don't even think about it. Besides, chocolate is bad for dogs, it can kill you. Just like I hope it will kill me." She drove back home.

She got a couple more manuscripts and spent the rest of the day poring over them. Around nine she pulled out her atlas and went to the Washington State map. She had decided to get out of town and start visiting the big cities around the area. Olympia was the closest. It was also the state capital. She decided to get up early and drive down there, look around, then come back before her party. It might take her mind off meeting the city officials and the lumberjacks that Lois was bringing.

She closed up her computer and went to the bedroom. Van Gogh was already on the bed. "Lazy dog, you'd probably let a burglar break in if it interrupted your sleep." She undressed and crawled under the covers. She was asleep shortly after.

Very early the next morning she was up and managed to make a good breakfast again. Van Gogh had been fed, and Sarah packed a little basket with sandwiches. "So we don't have to pay high prices for lunch," she told the dog. She got on her coat and decided to see if the dog would just follow her to the car, but she did take the retractable leash in case they explored. She picked up the basket and a bag with the leash and other needs for the road, like chocolate donuts.

Van Gogh was happy to be off the leash and went straight for the car. Sarah put the goodies in the back and got in after the dog jumped past her to the passenger seat. "Good, Van Gogh. You are a good puppy." She rolled down his window a bit, and he stuck his head out. She drove off and down the highway 101 South toward Olympia. Sarah hoped she would see Zeus or any of the other gods. She liked to dream about such romantic things.

She finally arrived in the city, and they had a good time exploring. She spent about five hours walking around sightseeing and then decided to head home. She had enough of the city. Country life was in her blood now. Besides, she wanted to get back before her party to have time to get ready. She said good-bye to Olympia, regretting that she saw no Greek gods.

By the time she got back to Brinnon, it was going on four, so she had three hours to make herself look presentable for the men. Yeah, right. She spent a little time getting ready and looked at Van Gogh.

Fatal Rejection

"Well, puppy, I'm sorry you can't go. This is for humans only. Now I hope you can be good and not tear apart the house. I don't want to lock you in a room, so roam and be good." Van Gogh just sat looking dumb. Sarah ruffled his head and went to the door. She looked back, and Van Gogh was still sitting in the living room. She was amazed and hoped that this was a good sign. She went out the door and drove to town.

She arrived at the VFW hall just out of town. The parking lot was busy. She was getting a bit nervous. So many cars, were they all here for her? She found a space close to the building and went in. She went through a small vestibule and then into a big room. She was shocked. They were all men! She was ready to run back out screaming when she heard Lois' voice in the crowd.

"Sarah! Over here!" She was waving to her. Sarah made her way through the men, all of them checking her out. She had decided to wear a tight black dress that showed off her great legs. She wanted to give the old men in the city council a heart attack. She found her way to Lois standing by a door.

"Sarah, you look fabulous! Come with me to the party."

"This isn't where it's at?" Sarah asked.

"Oh, heavens no, this is the VFW club room. These men are all veterans, but I'm sure they'd love to meet you, too. Maybe later." Lois pulled Sarah to the door. She was thankful she wasn't going to meet all the men in that room. Lois took her into the banquet hall, and Sarah went into a panic again. This room was filled with people also, and Sheriff Dave was sitting right up front, probably admiring her legs. She thought, "Please someone, put a bullet in my head."

*

Chapter 17

He stood looking at the dead body, amazed at what just happened. He had previously read in the papers about suspects dying while being tasered by policebefore he but didn't think it could happen with his lousy stun gun. He didn't know what to do now. He wasn't prepared for this. Should he tie her up and cut her throat? Since she was dead, there would be no blood spurting since the heart wasn't pumping anymore. The thrill was gone.

Just for the hell of it, he slit her throat, but he knew that the ME would say it was postmortem. He wanted to at least leave a calling card. He picked up his bag, quickly left the house and went back to his car. He was bordering on disappointment and anger, frustrated by the amount of time and trouble he went to for the kill only to have it wrenched from him by the stupid stun gun. He'd need to find a different way to incapacitate his victims.

He drove around the city until he came to an area where he could see hookers standing on the corners, hawking their wares. His blood was pounding in his veins from the adrenalin rush he had built up for the kill. He needed some release. He drove down the block a bit until he found one woman standing alone waving to him. He pulled up and rolled the window down.

"Hey, baby cakes, what about some adventure?" she said. The woman was not very attractive but her breasts were almost out of the tube top she wore. "I'm primo good fun. You like?"

"Get in," he said and unlocked the door.

She hopped in and said, "I don't kiss, except on the dick, and I don't do doggy. I need fifty for ten minutes, or I'm walking."

He smiled at her, drove off, then found a dark alley and turned into it. The alley was a dead end, but he didn't care. It was perfect for what he had in mind. He opened his door and got out, walking around to her side. He pulled open the door and reached in, grabbed her by the arm and yanked her out. She started to yell, but he slapped her so hard she went dazed. He dragged her to a pole holding a street lamp that wasn't working and pulled her arms behind her and around the pole, zip tying her wrists. She started to scream, and he hit her hard in the face.

He turned her away from his car, reached around with the knife he took from the sheath in his coat pocket and slit her throat. The blood splattered on the brick wall of the building she was facing. He didn't touch the blood, not sure if she had HIV or some other disease that would affect him. He stood back as she bled out, sliding down the pole until her ass was on the ground. He snapped a couple pictures with his cell phone, remembering that he forgot to take any at Warick's home. Oh, well.

He got into his car and backed out of the alley. He sped off in the direction of his hotel, feeling a little better but not entirely satisfied. In his room he stood looking at his reflection in the mirror, being sure he had no blood splatter on him. Satisfied, he went to his laptop and wrote his chapter on the newest murder of a prostitute. He mentioned that she was a prostitute so Sarah would know the killer wasn't after any particular people. This was different. He was killing indiscriminately, which gave him a thrill. Before, he had always gone after certain planned victims, but to just grab someone and kill gave him a rush.

Fatal Rejection

He was breathing harder and felt like he would explode. He went to the phone and called the concierge again. He needed release.

The next morning after he paid the hooker and sent her on her way, he packed and vacated his room. He wasn't very happy with the way things went, but not much he could do now; he had an agenda to fill. He went to the front desk and took care of the room, paying cash, then went to his car. He had a long ride ahead.

He was on day four of his trip and barely halfway to his destination. He arrived in Minneapolis after about seven hours of driving. He was not going to go much farther today. He had no plans to murder anyone here. He didn't research any book editors or agents in this city.

He checked into another cheap motel on the outskirts of the city and fired up his laptop. He checked his e-mail and found a couple from various fans, one from Max and one from another future writer named Charles Weaver. He read their letters and thought them over before replying. He received a reply from Sarah as he was sitting at the desk. It surprised him. He opened the e-mail. It was just corrections about his murder of the prostitute. Sarah put a note on the e-mail saying she was surprised that he mentioned her profession since he didn't say what the other women did. Derek felt by the way she wrote the note that she was being intrusive. He had his reasons, and it was none of her business. Besides it might give away his purpose too early. He never told Sarah that he was coming across country. As far as she was concerned, he was in his apartment at his desk writing.

He sent out his replies to his fans then closed down the laptop. He was tired from the drive. It was a boring country to go through, a strain on his mind. He went to the bed and stretched out after setting his alarm for two hours. He didn't have any plans for tonight, he might just watch television.

Two hours later his alarm stirred him from his nap and he got up feeling hungry. He changed his clothing and went out to the office of the motel.

"Excuse me," he asked of the bored looking clerk reading a magazine. The clerk barely looked up and asked what he wanted.

"Can you tell me where there is a decent seafood restaurant around here?"

"Well, there's Long John Silvers or the Fish Shack down the street. Otherwise I don't know of any others."

Derek frowned at the poor reception the clerk gave him and went out of the office without thanking him. "Damn rude people," he mumbled. "Maybe I should take him out, slit his throat while he reads his stinking magazine." The thought perked him up, but the killing would be too close to him so he thought better of it.

He drove around and found a seafood restaurant closer into the city. He stopped and had a nice sit down dinner complete with waiters and busboys, not fast food service. He sat after his meal and studied his notebook. He had dealings with an editor in Billings, Montana, since he had sent a submission of his first book there to a small publisher of outdoor books. He figured they wouldn't go for his book but he was sending out submissions to just about every publisher he could find. He received a rejection from this editor, too. She wasn't rude but wasn't helpful. He figured he'd give her the thrill of a visit.

He watched television the rest of the night, and around midnight he was getting restless. Minneapolis was a big city and maybe a drive around would do him some good. He got into his car and drove to the downtown of the city then made his way down side streets looking. Just looking, maybe for a hooker out alone, needing a lesson to be taught. Bad girl, you need a lesson from me, he thought.

About a half hour later he found what he was looking for. She was old for a prostitute, but she held up well. He pulled up, and she leaned on the car as Derek ran the window down.

"How much?" Derek asked.

"Whatcha want, honey?" She spoke with a hoarse voice. Either too many cigarettes or talks too much, Derek thought.

"Around the world," he replied, having heard the term before.

"Riding hard for the night? I can keep up if you can. Cost ya a c-note."

Derek pushed the button to unlock the door, and she got in. "You have a place we can go?" he asked.

"I got a room nearby. We can go there."

He followed her directions and arrived at another cheap motel. It was perfect, well hidden, and the rooms were separated from sight of the others. He could slip in and out without being seen. He parked his Caddie on the street away from the motel.

"You can park in the lot, you know," she said.

"I like to keep the car away from prying eyes."

"It's your c-note, whatever you want."

Derek got out of the car and pulled the bag out of his trunk. She gave him the eye and he said, "It's a change of clothing. Just in case."

She didn't understand and didn't care. She wanted the money. They walked to the motel and went into her room. She walked to the dresser and dropped her purse and jacket.

"Are you healthy, in good shape and your heart strong?" Derek asked as the hooker was unzipping her dress.

"Of course, honey. How do you think I've survived this long in this business?"

"Very good," Derek said, as he fired the stun gun.

*

Chapter 18

Lois pulled Sarah to the head table where Dave was sitting next to a younger man and a woman. Lois guided Sarah to a chair and picked up a wireless microphone.

"Attention everyone, quiet down, please. I want to introduce the newest member of our community, even if she does live way out in the boonies." That got a laugh. "She's living in the former Carlson house, and she came all the way from New York to join us." There were about fifty or so people in the room, a mixture of younger and older people. Most of them were couples with a few single men and women. Sarah was trying not to look at Dave, but she could see him next to her out of the corner of her eye. He was dressed nicely in a suit and tie. He looked good.

So, everyone, welcome Sarah Keller." Lois reached to Sarah and pulled her up from her chair as everyone was applauding. Sarah gave her best Queen Elizabeth wave and glanced at Dave. He was checking out her legs. She leaned to him and said quietly, "My face is up here, sport."

He blushed, looked up, then he smiled and went on applauding. Sarah had the microphone thrust at her and Lois said, "Tell us about yourself, dear," loud enough for the room to hear. Sarah had to take the mic.

"Uh…well…there's not much to say. I came from New York, the city, where I worked…still work…for a publishing company. I do my work now by computer and e-mail. It saves on the long drive." That got a laugh and Sarah relaxed. "I bought my home from Lois since she has the monopoly on real estate here, and I'm still settling in. I just got a dog. He's in charge of the house now. I haven't got used to country life yet. I'm still waiting to hear the police and fire sirens every twenty minutes. And I have yet to see a Yellow Cab." The group was laughing now, and Sarah was enjoying it. "I've never lived near a huge river like the Hood Canal. We had sewers in New York that would back up every so often, and sometimes the children would open up a fire plug and create a fountain. That's the most water I was exposed to. Well, that's enough about me. Enjoy yourselves, and I hope to be able to meet all of you."

She handed the mic back to Lois who continued, "Johnny Cee is going to be our D.J. for the dancing. Please stop by to introduce yourselves to Sarah." She turned off the microphone and sat. The couple at the table were introduced by Lois. "Sarah, this is Ken Harris, our mayor, and his wife, Janet." Sarah was surprised that the mayor was so young. She acknowledged them as a few more people came over to say their hellos. She was busy greeting people. They all were very friendly and nice. Lois finally introduced her to Harold, her younger boyfriend. Sarah thought he looked nice for a kept man.

The D.J. looked like he was barely out of high school. He had his records set up next to a turntable with speakers on both ends of the table. Sarah had to laugh remembering the D.J.s in the clubs back in New York with their thousands of dollars in equipment. But she had to admit the boy was good as he started off.

She finally turned to Dave sitting quietly beside her. "How are you doing?" she asked politely.

"Well, it's good to have a night off from crime fighting."

"Who's guarding the town, Mike?"

"Yes, he is. He may be young, but he's efficient and does whatever I tell him, which is handy."

"So you put him out patrolling while you sit in the donut shop?"

"We don't have a donut shop, just the Halfway House. I sit there eating their donuts and drinking coffee. Mike takes care of crime."

"Well, I have to say you look nice out of your uniform," Sarah said with a smile.

"I'm not often out of my uniform other than when I'm in bed."

"Alone, I presume," Sarah said, again with a smile.

"That's a little personal. Do you go to bed alone?"

"No, I have a man in my bed now."

Dave looked a little perplexed. Sarah laughed and said, "My dog. Van Gogh."

Fatal Rejection

"Van Gogh, the painter?"

"Yes, he has a small chunk of his ear missing, so I named him Van Gogh."

"Why don't you call him Vincent?"

"I like Van Gogh better. Vincent reminds me of Vincent Price, the horror actor. He scares me."

"The dog could protect you."

"Yes, he could and would."

Johnny the D.J. put on a recording by the Righteous Brothers from the sixties, "Ebb Tide." Dave paused and then asked, "Are you averse to dancing?"

She looked to the dance floor. It was busy so she would be lost in the crowd. "No, are you asking?"

"Yes." She pushed her chair back with help from Dave and they went to the floor. He didn't get in too close since he knew she was not ready for that sort of thing. Sarah could smell his cologne. It was very appealing. "What fragrance are you wearing?"

He smiled and said, "Black Suede by Avon."

Sarah about choked. "Avon? You get Avon out here, and you buy it?"

"Yes, I do. My neighbor, Lilly France, sells it and always catches me at the door with her products. I try to keep her happy by buying something. My bathroom is full of Avon products." He could feel her laughing silently.

"Is this Lilly cute?" she asked.

"She's in her late sixties and married. So you don't have to worry."

"I wasn't worrying. You're free to keep any woman happy by buying her products. I may have some land to sell you."

"Lois wouldn't like that."

"I've decided to give her competition by becoming a Realtor."

"She may kill you in your sleep. The last woman to try that did die in her sleep. We still haven't proven it was Lois."

Sarah looked up at him and said, "I hope you're kidding."

He just smiled and spun her around the dance floor. Johnny started to play another slow song. It

Fatal Rejection

was "From This Moment" by Shania Twain. Sarah just kept moving to the music. Dave finally moved a bit closer to her, and she put her head on his chest. She was feeling mixed emotions. This felt so good and it had been so long. The only men she had even hugged were at Sean's funeral and her male co-workers at her going away party from her company. Those were friendly hugs. This felt different. A bit warmer, and she felt a tingle at the base of her spine as Dave moved his hand down her back.

She moved closer to him, into a tighter embrace, swaying to the romantic song by Shania, one about loving forever. She listened to the song and thought how she and Sean never had a favorite first dance song. They had eloped, so there was no wedding dance even. Was this going to be one of those favorite songs for her and Dave?

The song ended and they both paused a moment before breaking the hold. Dave cleared his throat and guided Sarah back to the table. Lois gave Sarah a sly smile. Sarah leaned to Lois and said, "It was just a dance."

Lois said quietly, "You know what they say about dancing. It's the vertical prelude to horizontal love."

"Lois! Stop that, it's nothing. Just a dance," she said, but wondered if it meant more. Dave had gone off to get drinks for them. Sarah watched him from across the room at the open bar. She remembered her feelings about getting involved with a cop. He could get killed anytime. She didn't need that.

He returned and gave her the drink she had asked for. After about three more drinks, she didn't care if he was a cop or a mailman. Everyone finally dies. She watched him talking to the mayor and laughing. He was very handsome in a rugged sort of way. She was getting light-headed and giddy. Another slow dance came on, and she pulled him to the dance floor. They embraced and she nuzzled his neck. He was enjoying it. The D.J. announced that the night had come to an end, the VFW needed the room for their dancing now.

Sarah stood, taking the microphone. "I just want to say that I enjoyed meeting all of you. Thank you for welcoming me to your community." Everyone applauded her. She staggered a little, and Dave steadied her. "I think I better drive you home," he said quietly. "I don't want to have to arrest you for drunk driving."

She put her arms around his neck. "Carry me to your car," she said, slurring her words slightly.

"Oh no, not here in front of all these people. You will walk out on your own with your head up. No sense letting everyone see how you are when you drink."

Fatal Rejection

"You got it, flatfoot. I'll walk out with my head up and you'll help me walk straight. Won't you?"

He smiled and led her out the door just as the veterans were all flowing into the room. She saw Lois leaving with Harold, and she waved and said have a nice evening.

He got her to his Bronco and poured her into the vehicle. She didn't protest. He drove her to her home and got her to the door. She was coming around a little with the fresh air. "Where's my car?"

"I'll get it to you in the morning. Now go in and go to bed." She fumbled for her keys as she heard the dog barking.

"Oh, that's Van Gogh. He's been good, I hope." She opened the door, and the dog came flying out and jumped up around her. Dave pointed her in the direction of the living room, and she went to the couch and collapsed. He stood next to the dog. They were both looking at her. "Keep an eye on her, Van Gogh. I'll let myself out."

*

Chapter 19

Derek felt better about himself. Casual killing was coming easier to him. He now understood what the Slasher was about. He randomly killed women in each city he went to. Derek didn't know if the Slasher had any kind of plan. All the kills seemed random, so he assumed that the Slasher just picked his victims from what was available. Not like how Derek started out with his desire to murder editors and agents. His kills were planned in advance.

He had a new taste for blood, and this latest hooker opened new feelings for him. He left her on the bed, spread eagled just like his third victim in Buffalo, the book editor he lured to the motel. It was after 2 a.m., and he was crashing from the high he got with the hooker's demise. He made his way back to his motel and didn't even open the laptop. He wanted to be fresh for the extra-long drive to Billings, Montana. He crashed on the bed, clothes and all. He was asleep quickly and had pleasant dreams.

According to his calculations it would take about 12 hours of straight driving to get to Billings, so he plotted his stops for rest and food using the map he had with him. He was just past Bismarck, North Dakota, half way to his next destination, when stopped for lunch at a roadside diner. The food was good, and the waitress was sassy and funny. He thought maybe he'd come back there one day.

On the road again, he drove straight through until he made the border of Billings. He found a motel, a nice one this time, and checked in. He fired up his laptop and checked his e-mail. Nothing important, just the two pests Max and Charles asking for more advice and information on his next book. He was polite but brief in his replies. Nothing from Sarah, but he hadn't sent in a new chapter yet. He spent about an hour and a half typing up the story of the Minneapolis hooker's death and sent it to Sarah. That should throw her off his plan, another random kill.

He opened up the Google page and checked for his next victim, Rachel Harris. She was an editor for Black Hill Publishing, one that he had sent his submission to years back. He pulled out his cell phone, called the company and asked for her. The person who answered said she was off this week on vacation. Derek panicked.

"Has she left the city?" he asked.

"No, she's staying home to renovate. She's such a busy person," the person replied. "Did you have a reason to see her?"

"I'm looking for someone to free-lance an edit of my next book, and she was recommended. Thank you for the information," he said and hung up before she could ask any more questions.

He had an address for her home so he looked up the location on his city map from the Atlas he carried. He found the street and went to his car. He got lost a couple times and had to re-check the map. He finally found the street and drove slowly down looking for the house. It was a very secluded house on the edge of the desert range. The nearest neighbor was almost a quarter mile from Harris' home. Perfect.

Should he go in now or wait until darkness? He debated. He drove by the house again and saw only one car in the long dusty driveway, so he pulled in. He got out of his car. It was hot so he removed his jacket, putting his knife in his back pants pocket, just in case. He figured on leaving the stun gun in the car until he knew the situation, then he would make an excuse to go get it.

He walked up to the door and knocked. He waited, and the door was opened by a rather smallish woman with long pigtails running down over breasts outlined by a t-shirt that was a bit tight. She looked to be Mexican or Native American by her skin tone and features.

"Hola, may I help you?" she asked with an accent he thought to be Mexican.

"Are you Rachel Harris?"

Fatal Rejection

"I am, and you are?"

"I'm Derek Harcourt, the author of 'The Killing Machine,' a book about the NY Slasher."

"Yes, Mr. Harcourt, I have heard of you. Is there something I can do for you?"

"I'm looking for someone to edit my next book. I'm not happy with the one I have now. Would you be interested?"

"Why me?" she asked with a slight questioning look.

"I prefer a free-lance editor and I've heard good things about you. Can we talk, if I'm not disturbing any guests you may have?"

"No, I'm alone right now. My boyfriend had to work today. I guess we could at least talk. Come in."

"Oh, thank you, but I need my case from the car if you can wait a moment. It has my papers."

"Sure, go get them. I'd like to read what you have."

Derek smiled and went back to the car to get his bag and the stun gun. All was going well with this one.

Back at the motel, Derek opened the bottle of 18 year-old Glenfiddich Scotch he carried with him and poured out a generous portion into the motel drinking glass. He went back to the laptop and finished writing the newest chapter of the murder in Montana. Nice name for a book, if he ever got around to it. The Billings woman was an easy target, a sitting duck so to speak. But Derek was starting to have a desire for the ones that were harder to get. The women who walked the streets intrigued him. They were street smart and could be tough, but being careful could result in a good kill.

He was becoming a hunter, and the streets were his hunting grounds with the prey hiding in the brush. Maybe later tonight he would go out for a good hunt, that is, if Billings had any hookers. He finished the chapter and sent it off to Sarah. Lovely Sarah, how he would rejoice in her capture. Did she suspect that he had anything to do with the murder of her husband and her best friend?

He found out after he killed Sean Keller that he was painting a portrait of Sarah's friend Betsy Clark to give her husband. Derek had interrupted them and tried to make the murder look like a lover's spat gone very wrong. The police figured it out though. The angles of the cuts gave it away. They said an unknown assailant committed the crime.

Fatal Rejection

Oh, well, it must have made Sarah very upset when she got home and found the two of them in bed with all that blood around them. He could just imagine the hurt she felt at the loss, kind of like how he felt when she sent that hateful letter to him about his book.

But he would have his revenge. It was coming close now. He was over half way there, and in two days he would be finishing his book with his final kill. Then maybe he'd disappear like his hero. Where would he go? He could resurrect Eugene Petrovskia and live quietly back in Bismarck, North Dakota, near that diner with the sassy waitress. She was single, or so she kept telling Derek, and she was good looking. He would have to curb his murderous feelings, but could he? There were no hookers in Bismarck, as far as he knew, but if he was going to be off the grid, he'd have to give it up.

He finished the chapter and sent it off to Sarah. The Internet was a wondrous thing. He could hide anywhere in the United States and make her think he was thousands of miles away in New York. He had a plan to tease her when he arrived in Seattle, but he would have to explore the city first. It was huge and filled with a life that had its own style. He didn't want to mar his visit with a kill that he wanted to savor. A full day in Seattle, then a day with Sarah. It was going to be a nice finish to his quest.

Chapter 20

Van Gogh sat patiently staring at Sarah, prone on the couch, snoring loudly. His patience was wearing thin. He barked loudly close to her head. It caused her to suddenly sit up straight in a panic.

"What the hell? Ow!" she said, grabbing her head. She looked around, then down to Van Gogh. "Oh no, what did I do last night? Did I make a fool of myself? I knew I shouldn't have had those Fuzzy Navels. They always mess me up." She swung her legs around to the floor. Van Gogh moved away so not to get stepped on. She stood shakily and went to the front door, opened it and looked out.

"Van Gogh, where is my car?" she said, half expecting the dog to answer. He didn't. She turned and nearly ran into the door. "Damn, I hate the morning after. Van Gogh, did I sleep with anyone, like Dave?" He said nothing again. She went to the phone and called the sheriff's office. Mike answered.

"Hi, is Sheriff Chandler in?" she asked.

"He's out on the road on a mission. He'll be back in an hour," the deputy said.

Fatal Rejection

"Would you tell him that Sarah Keller called?"

"Sure, Mrs. Keller, but he's on his way out to your house."

"Oh, I didn't know that. I'll watch for him, thank you." She hung up and went to the front door to look out again. She sat on the porch steps, still holding her head. Van Gogh followed her out, came up next to her and put his head on her lap. She smiled and petted him. Then he ran off to do his business.

About five minutes later two cars drove into her drive, one her car driven by Dave. She didn't know who was in the second car. They parked and Dave got out of her car and waved to her. She grimaced a smile and stood.

"Hey, you survived. Head a little big this morning?" Dave said as he approached.

"Did you do anything to me last night?" she asked.

He laughed and said, "I wish, but no. I drove you home and left you on the couch. I was a gentleman and didn't undress you either."

She looked down and realized she still had on the tight dress. She stood, went back into the door and grabbed a long coat from the vestibule rack. She came back out and up to Dave. "Thank you for your discretion. I'm not a big drinker."

"I could see that. I'll remember it also. So I brought back your car. Virgil drove out with me to take me back to town." He pointed to the man in the second car. The man waved. "Virgil is a friend and was hanging around the sheriff's office so I put him to work, which I have to go back to. I hope you feel better soon." He smiled and turned to go to his friend's car.

She called to him, "If you have some time later, can you stop by?"

He looked back and said, "Sure. What time?"

"Anytime. I'm not going anywhere today."

"Yeah, I imagine you won't." He smiled, got in Virgil's car, and they drove off.

She went back inside, followed by Van Gogh. "Are you sure he didn't take advantage of me?" she asked the dog. He didn't answer.

"Smart dog. Don't rat out the cop." She went to the kitchen to get something in her stomach. She totally scorched the toast and blackened the eggs. She threw it all out in the garbage and went back to the couch. She lay there feeling a little disappointed that he didn't take advantage of her. Then he could have stayed for breakfast and made his great pancakes. They would have spent a relaxing soak in the tub, drinking wine and playing footsie. The thought of wine started her head hurting again. She blanked her mind and went back to sleep.

About an hour later her phone rang. She fell off the couch, crawled to the phone, and pulled it off the desk by the cord. She fumbled around on the floor looking for it and yelling for the person to hold on. She found it and held up the receiver. "Hello?"

It was Lois. Now her head started hurting again and not from the drinks. "Yes, Lois?"

"Dear, how was your night?" she asked.

"Not like you would have hoped. I passed out on the couch and that's all I remember. I'm not much of a drinker."

"Well, you did polish off a number of them last night," she said with a laugh.

"Did I embarrass myself?"

"Oh, heavens, no. You didn't look like you were drunk until you got to the parking lot. Harold and I watched Dave put you in his car and drive off. Did he stay the night?"

"No, he was a gentleman and deposited me on my couch and left."

"Oh, well, there will be other nights."

"Lois, stop. I don't want a romance." She was starting to lie to herself now. She thoroughly enjoyed being with Dave at the party last night.

"Okay, dear. I'll just let nature run its course." She laughed again and hung up.

"I'm living in loony central," she said to Van Gogh. He wagged his tail and tried to lick her face as she lay on the floor with the phone still in her hand. She pushed him aside and hung up the phone. Sitting up, she felt a little better. She got up and sat at her desk, starting up her computer. There was nothing from New York, but there was one from Harcourt. She started to read it to try and get her eyes in focus. She realized that Harcourt gave his victims an occupation, hooker. "Well, Derek, you're finally starting to tell us your desire. Are you a fan of hookers, or is this just a random hit?"

"Van Gogh, we have hookers now. Shall we celebrate?" He didn't respond, just closed his eyes and snorted from the floor.

"Okay, sleep, I don't care. You're no fun anymore. And I'm still a little high. Wow, that is not something I want to do again. Or at least only in moderation."

She finished her corrections and put a little note about the women being hookers. She sent it back to Derek in New York. She wondered what was going on out there in the Big Apple. She stood and went to take off the coat and change into more respectable clothes. She thought about going out for lunch, but she didn't feel up to driving. She forced herself to make lunch or they would find a skinny dead body in the house. Ham again, yum. Van Gogh had his dog food, and she was sitting on the couch eating her sandwich when the doorbell rang.

"Crap, never any rest." She got up and went to the door, opening it. Her heart jumped a bit. It was Dave.

"Oh, hello, Sheriff. What brings you out here again?"

"Uh, you invited me," he said with that great smile of his.

"Yes, I guess I did. Come in. I didn't expect you so soon."

"I put Mike in charge and came back to see if you were all right. And to find out what you wanted."

"What I wanted? Yes…I did say I wanted you to come back. Let me think for what."

He was trying not to laugh, but she was so damn cute. He moved closer to her and she looked up at him.

"Oh, hell," she said and grabbed onto him with a big, slow, sloppy kiss. He didn't resist. He pulled her in tightly with his arms around her. She was lost in his lips, tasting them and feeling alive again.

She pushed back and apologized. "I'm sorry. I don't know what came over me. It probably was the alcohol."

"Well, I'm not sorry," he said as he moved to her and pulled her back, kissing her tenderly. This time she didn't resist.

They were like two teenagers making out, then she realized where they were. Sarah pulled back again and was feeling the heat of the kiss. Dave was standing, wanting more.

"Let's take this slow, please. I'm confused. My feelings haven't changed, but I'm terribly attracted to you. Can we go slowly with this?"

"I'm fine with that. You tell me where you want to take it. I'll follow you anywhere."

Fatal Rejection

She smiled and said, "It's only two o'clock. Can you come back later tonight around seven, and we can discuss this then?"

"I can do that. Are you sure this is what you want? I'm still recovering from a broken romance, and you are smarting from your past."

"Yes, come back and we'll just talk about the boundaries we will need for this. Go now, please, before I do something dumb."

He turned towards the door and then looked back, smiled and said, "I'll be here for you."

He left, and she started to hyperventilate. She went to her kitchen and turned on the water. She ran her hands under it and splashed her face with the cold liquid. She wanted to take a very cold shower but she hated cold showers. She was hot now and she liked it. That man brought out something in her that she hadn't felt in a long time. She went to the mantle over the fireplace in the living room where she had placed the picture of her and Sean.

She took the picture down. "Sean, I loved you greatly, and I will always have you in my heart, but I have to go on. I hope you understand." She kissed the picture and put it back on the mantle.

*

Chapter 21

Derek was packed and on his way out I-90 towards Butte, then on to Spokane, Washington. His adrenaline was spiking from the thought of getting so close to his goal. He had to reel in his excitement. He was going to take a little time to relax later in Seattle before he made his way around the Hood Canal to Brinnon, Washington, where Sarah had her new home. Canal was a misnomer. It was more of a natural waterway with Seattle far off in the east and Brinnon on the west.

He drove out the highway barely paying any attention to the scenery, lost in thought about what he was going to do to her. He had studied her home through Google maps, using the satellite mode. Fantastic device. He could see all the property around the house and all the way into town. He checked out the landscape for hiding places and the coast of the Hood Canal for approaching the house without being seen. He knew the nearest house was far enough away to be oblivious to the kill. Yes, he loved Google maps and satellite spying.

He had driven about four hours from Butte, and he knew he was about three hours from Seattle. He was tired of trying to find a radio station that wouldn't fade, so he just shut the thing off. He hummed to himself a tune that was stuck in his head from the radio, "Xanadu" by Olivia Newton John. It kept rolling through his head until he turned the radio back on to listen to static.

He arrived in Spokane and stopped to get lunch. He found a restaurant that promised home cooking even though he remembered that his mother was a lousy cook. She nearly poisoned him with a stroganoff that had mushrooms from the backyard. She was a good woman, just a drunk with a violent temper, especially with that asshole of a husband. But he didn't have to worry about either of them now.

He didn't have the stroganoff, but the meal was good and he was happy. He got back on the road, and after three hours he could see Seattle in his sights. He had already found a motel on the Internet and drove to it by way of the directions from Google. After parking, he went in and registered for a room. The place had Wi-Fi so he could hook up his laptop.

In his room he arranged his bags and clothes. He was going to be there a few days, even after he did the deed with Sarah. It was his final stop, and he planned on making the best of it. He wasn't even going to think about the trip back to New York. Maybe he'd just stay here.

He fired up his laptop and checked his e-mail. One letter from Charles. He was surprised that Max hadn't bothered him yet, but the day was young. He received a reply from Sarah about his last kill. She questioned the change in the serial killer's murders to hookers. She knew about serial killers' habits, and they rarely diverted from the M.O. they had. He ignored her question and figured she would let it go.

Derek didn't care. He was going to get out of the writing business after this week. He was growing weary of the whole mess, too many experts online telling him how to write and picking at his book. Why didn't they just read the damn thing and enjoy the plot without picking at the unimportant things like grammar and tenses? Damn word Nazis.

He shut down his e-mail program and opened up Google to check out the night life in Seattle. He enjoyed jazz, and there were a good number of jazz clubs in town. Tomorrow he would go up in the Space Needle to look out over the city, and maybe he would be able to see Brinnon across the lake. He wished he had binoculars, something he should have for spying on his victims. Of course, if he was going to continue to murder random hookers, he really didn't need binoculars. They liked to get close up in your face.

He had time so he turned on the television to see what the news had to say. He liked watching the news. It had all the good crimes to report. The anchor sat at the desk with his combed over hair looking silly. Derek laughed. The man was talking about the city wide search for a killer who was attacking prostitutes, having murdered four in the last week. Derek perked up hearing this. Damn, he had a competitor. Not good if he wanted to grab a lady of the streets to satisfy his needs. Now the police would be watching every car in search of a hooker. He just couldn't stand someone stealing his thunder. This just sucked.

The anchor talked about the string of murders across the country with the FBI now involved. They were saying that the NY Slasher might be back in business, but there was no proof it was him. Derek smiled at the connection to his murders being blamed on the Slasher. No one would be looking for Derek Harcourt. He was not a suspect, and no one even knew where he was. He was carefully covering his tracks. Eugene Petrovskia was the man they would look for if they suspected him, not Derek.

Derek sat wondering if it was even a good idea to go out, but the thought of a jazz bar appealed to him, so he changed clothes and went down to his car. He had a Google list printed of the clubs he could go to, so he was ready to enjoy himself even if he couldn't take out a hooker.

Derek had just hit the third club, not happy with the clientele or the bands in the first two, and sat at the bar. The female drink jockey took his order, and he relaxed, watching the combo on the small stage doing their best with Dave Brubeck music. Derek liked Brubeck so he felt good about this place. There were also fewer people so he wasn't distracted by the crowd, and they were well behaved. He was grooving to "Take Five" when he heard a voice next to him.

"You like Brubeck?" a woman said to him. She was very good looking and had long dark hair around her slim shoulders. She looked to be about his age, maybe around thirty-five, but he was not good at judging ages.

Derek was a little surprised that a woman would try to pick him up. He was a good looking man and was well dressed so he didn't look like some rummy off the streets. He smiled at her and turned his stool and his attentions to her.

"I do like Brubeck. It's odd a woman would. Do you like jazz?"

"Yes, I do. My father got me into jazz. He picked a mean bass for a couple jazz bands in his day. I even got to meet Brubeck when I was younger."

"Well, that's fortunate. I'm jealous. I live in New York and have heard a good number of jazz bands. I even watched Woody Allen and his jazz band once in New Orleans."

"That must have been fun. Are you in town for business?"

Fatal Rejection

"That and pleasure. I've never been to the city, so I made it an objective to come here."

"What do you do?"

"I'm a writer, murder novels. Well, I have only one so far, but that's why I'm here. I'm researching my second book."

"Well, murders. You aren't killing all the hookers in Seattle, are you?" She laughed.

"Goodness, no. I murder on paper. I leave the real stuff to the serial killers out there. Aren't you afraid to be out on the street? I notice there are not many women walking around tonight."

"I live in this building, upstairs, so I don't have to go out," she said with a big smile.

"Then you must get to hear all the good jazz."

"I do. Would you like to come up and give a listen?" she said with a sly smile.

Derek didn't say anything but smiled. She slid off her stool, took him by the hand and led him out of the club. She went to an open elevator in the building's hallway and pulled him in, hitting a button for the second floor. The doors closed, and she went at him with a passion that he didn't resist.

The elevator stopped at the second floor, and she pulled him to an apartment where she unlocked the door and they went in. Derek regretted not having his bag but he figured he could make do with what he found in the apartment. This was turning out to be a good night.

*

Chapter 22

Sarah went about her business cleaning her house. She felt domestic for the first time in a long while. She opened the door to the second bedroom, saw the boxes still piled up and closed the door.

"Not today, Van Gogh," she told the dog who had been following her around. She took a vacuum from the closet in the utility room and brought it out. Van Gogh saw the machine and ran off towards the bedrooms. "Coward!" she yelled after him. She did the living room and a few other carpet covered places, then put it away. Van Gogh came back out from his hiding.

She went to the kitchen and looked at the clock on the wall. It was just after five. She had two hours before he would be back. She decided to take a long warm bath so went to the bathroom but closed the dog out. She could hear him sniffing at the bottom of the door and yelled, "Go lie down, dog. I'm busy." He stopped.

She stripped down and felt the water she had running. It was just perfect. She had put in some bath oils to make her feel good. She hoped later she would feel better, but she wasn't going to get her hopes too high.

She slid down into the tub and let her aching body unwind. She was relaxing when she heard the phone ring. "Crap, the answering machine can get it. I'm not moving. I don't care for whatever Lois has for me now." She could hear the machine from the bathroom. It was Denise calling about her stories. She wanted to know if she could drop them off. She said she'd call back later and hung up.

Sarah soaked for about twenty-five minutes then got out before she totally pruned up. A wrinkled woman didn't look good if she was under seventy years old. She toweled off and threw the towel in the hamper, opened the door to the bedroom and nearly tripped over Van Gogh sleeping at the door.

"Damn, you're going to kill me one day," she said as he jumped up and went out of the room. She dressed in casual clothing, nothing too provocative for Dave's visit. She went out and found the dog by the back door. Potty time. She was amazed that the dog didn't seem to need to go out too often. He was probably stock piling his poop in some corner of the house for her to find. She opened the door and said, "Don't forget to come back."

She looked at the clock again. It was almost six-thirty. Her heart jumped a bit thinking about what she wanted to say to him. She was better at last minute doing than planning. She heard a bark and let the dog back in. "Wipe your feet," she said and closed the door. She looked out at the water again. It was calm, relaxing her nerves. She stood there for a moment then went to her desk to check her e-mail. She had two from New York, nothing from Harcourt. She shut down the computer. No work this evening, she thought. Only pleasure, she hoped.

Van Gogh was sleeping next to her desk when the doorbell rang. She looked at the clock. It was precisely seven. She had to say, the man was punctual. She went to the door and took in a deep breath then opened it and found him standing there.

"You know, I was standing out here for about ten minutes, debating whether to ring the bell or not," he said. "Not that I didn't want to, but I was worried about what you were going to say."

"Well, come in and find out." She smiled.

He came in and Van Gogh went right to him, sniffing his legs. "He probably smells the cat. Not really my cat. My girlfriend left him when she left. I prefer the cat now." He moved closer to her, and she gave him a shy look. He lifted her chin and gave her a small kiss on the lips. "Now, you wanted to talk?"

She turned and went to the living room, sitting on the couch. She patted the couch and said to join her. He did.

"Okay, I came out here to get away from the memories of my murdered husband. Have you ever seen crime scenes of brutally murdered bodies?"

"When I was on the PD in Tacoma, yes, I went to a number of bloodied scenes."

"Then you can understand what I went through finding my husband and best friend together in bed all cut up."

He just watched her. Best to let her get it all out.

She continued, "I found out later from the police that the whole thing must have been staged, but by whom, they didn't know. Nevertheless, my husband was still dead. I hurt very badly for a long time. He was my life back then. We had plans for a family and a good life. He had a safe occupation, painting, and he was good at it. Someday I'll show you the paintings I still have. I couldn't sleep or eat for so long. I had to get away. I decided to run as far as I could from the memories and came here. From one coast to the other, as far as possible without leaving the country, which I had thought about."

She stopped and asked, "Would you like something to drink? Water or soda? I'm not having any alcohol for a long while, but I need a drink."

"Sure, that would be nice. I'm a little dry. I'll take a can of soda. That would be nice."

She got up and went to the kitchen. Van Gogh came over and put his head on Dave's knee. Dave laughed and petted him. Sarah returned with two cans of Pepsi and gave one to Dave. She laughed at the dog resting on Dave and sat back in her seat. Van Gogh went back to his resting spot.

She took a big swig of the drink then paused. "Since I've been out here, I feel like I'm in a dream or a different world. New York and the murders are fading but not forgotten. I am just getting to like myself again…and you are helping. I'll admit that when Lois was trying to throw us together, I resisted. I don't like to be pushed. But the more I saw you, the more I wanted to get to know you better. I'm not saying I want a romance with you. Maybe, but I don't know right now. I'm feeling this thing…something that is making me weak when I'm around you. So we need to set boundaries if we are going to go on like this. Is this making any sense?"

Fatal Rejection

He grinned and said, "It does, I'm a little leery of getting too close again, so I understand. But I'm finding it hard to be near you without grabbing on to you and smothering you with kisses."

Sarah felt her cheeks getting hot. She must have blushed. "I have one problem. It's your occupation. You are a police officer and everyday there is a chance you could be shot and killed. I really don't think I could go through losing another man in my life." She paused to let this sink in.

"Well, the last shoot out we had in these parts was when Mort Rucker got drunk and shot up his ex-wife's house. He passed out before we got there. This is not the big city. We don't have drive-by shootings or robbers shooting up a store. It's a quiet little community that has a murder once every twenty years. I'm also careful about anything that looks dangerous. I'm no fool and don't want to be dead either." He paused to let it sink in.

"So, where are we in this?" Sarah asked.

Dave sat looking into her eyes and leaned forward, kissing her full on the lips. She responded by putting her arms around his neck and pulling him closer to her. They made out on the couch for a long while until Van Gogh came over and stuck his cold nose on Sarah's arm. She jumped causing Dave to fall back.

"Van Gogh! Stop that," she said, rubbing her arm.

"Think he's jealous?" Dave laughed.

"I'm wondering if he's just a dog. Sometimes he's too smart for his own good." She looked back at Dave and said, "Shall we go somewhere that's more private?"

"Lead the way," he said.

She stood and pulled him up, taking him to the bedroom, being sure to close the door with the dog outside.

Van Gogh huffed again at the door and turned a few times then plopped down, putting his head on his front paws.

Later that night around two a.m. Dave's cell phone buzzed. He reached down to his shirt and took the phone from the pocket. "This better be good," he said into the phone. He listened for a moment and said he'd be right there. He rolled back towards Sarah where she lay resting on her stomach and said, "I'm sorry, but Mike had a couple drunks from the VFW start a fight and he's having problems with them. I have to go help him." He sat up and started dressing. "But I will return as soon as they are safely in their cells. I'll make you my famous pancakes in the morning."

"You better or I'll come looking for you," she said.

He left the room, and she sighed. "The life of a cop's girlfriend."

*

Chapter 23

As soon as Derek was in the woman's apartment he said, "You haven't told me your name."

"I'm sorry, how rude of me. It's Sophia Palmira. And yes, I'm Italian. Please sit. Would you like some wine? I noticed you were drinking it at the bar."

"I usually drink Scotch, but tonight I just felt like a good Port with my jazz." He was intrigued by this woman. She was intelligent and, as he looked around her apartment, he could see she was well read. There were book shelves on three walls filled with many different novels from classics to crime. He was looking for his book but she came up with the glass of wine.

He had to ask, "Have you ever read 'The Killing Machine' by Derek Harcourt?"

She went to a shelf, looked at the many books and pulled out his book. He was surprised. She handed it to him and he opened it, pulled his pen from his pocket and signed it. She was watching him and was surprised.

"I hope you're Harcourt or I'll be upset."

"Yes, I have to confess, I am Derek Harcourt. I'm surprised you have my book."

"As you can see, I read a lot." She said with a smile.

He knew he could do her no harm now. She was special. He watched her put the book back on the shelf. She came back to him and said, "I've never personally known a famous author. You are the first."

"Well, I've never met a woman who has my book on her shelves. You are the first for me, too."

She took his glass from his hand and put it on the snack bar by the kitchen then put her arms around his neck. She kissed him carefully, not pushing or moving too fast. Soft slow kisses she gave him. He didn't resist.

She pulled him to her bedroom, and they stood facing each other as she worked his clothing off of him. She stood back in the low light of a table lamp and dropped her clothing. He watched her with great anticipation and a hot desire for her. The hookers he had the last week couldn't compare to the woman standing before him. She stood as a goddess, a woman to be put up and praised. Her body was perfect, rounded breasts and tight waist. She came close to him. He felt his privates growing hard. She pushed him back to the bed as they went into a passionate embrace and made fantastic love that night, all night.

It was about six in the morning when he felt her getting out of bed. He knew the time because she had a very large glowing clock on the wall across from the foot of the bed. Odd place he thought, but maybe she liked knowing what time it was.

She was in the bathroom for about a half hour then came out all dressed, conservatively.

"Well, I'd say you were going into an office job," Derek said from the bed.

She came around to his side of the bed and kissed him, then said, "Yes, I have a heavy schedule today. Just let yourself out."

"You never did say what occupation you were in."

"We hardly talked, did we? I'm a prosecuting attorney for the Seattle District Court."

The words sent a chill through Derek. This woman could put him in prison. She stood, giving him a strange smile, then she turned and went out of the bedroom. She yelled from the other room, "Don't let me find out you went through my underwear drawer." Then he heard a laugh and the door close.

He lay back on the bed thinking about this woman, so perfect but now dangerous to his health. He got out of the bed and dressed. Too bad, he thought. He was just getting to like her.

He left the building and found his car still parked at the curb in front of the building. It had a ticket under the wiper. He wasn't sure if this was good or bad. Bad for him, good for her. If he murdered Sophia now, the ticket would tie him to it. She was lucky on so many levels. He liked her enough to let her live, and the ticket could be his downfall. He'd see how things would go with her. Maybe he would be back, or not.

He drove back to his motel and checked his e-mail. Nothing from Sarah. Maybe she was busy. He read the two messages from Max and Charles, sent out terse replies and closed the laptop. He had no murder to write about. He might have to fall back on his imagination to write this next chapter.

He was well rested from his stay at Sophia's apartment so he didn't feel the need to rest at all. He paced the room thinking about his plans for the day. He had wanted to visit the Space Needle, a leftover from the Seattle World's Fair back in 1962 that stood 605 feet at its highest point. He stood staring out the window of his room. He could see the tower in the distance. The idea of going to the top made him feel like a little kid. He changed his clothes from last night, took a quick shower, and dressed casually for his adventure. He left the room and went to Seattle Center to go to the heavens.

Derek explored the city after reaching the restaurant towards the top of the tower. He had a nice lunch and then came back down to earth.

He was just heading back to his motel when his cell phone rang. It surprised him as he couldn't figure who would be calling him. He pulled it from his pocket and looked at the caller ID. It said *private*. He debated whether to answer, but pushed the button and said, "Hello?"

"Derek, this is Sophia. I'm not interrupting you, am I?"

He almost steered off the road when he heard her voice. "No, you're not interrupting. How did you get my number?"

She paused. "I hope you don't think it was rude of me. Your jacket was on the floor so I picked it up, and your card case fell out. I took one of the cards, and that's how I got your number. You aren't upset with me, are you?"

He thought quickly. "No, that's alright. It's not like I'm hiding anything."

"Oh, so you don't have a wife back home?" She laughed.

"No, there's not many woman who would want to marry a man who writes about serial killers."

"Speaking about that, do you think you'd have time to talk with me about serial killers? Our police are not having much luck catching the person responsible for the murder of the hookers in the city. I thought maybe you'd be able to give a friend of mine a few pointers."

"Who's your friend?" Derek was worried now.

"Detective Matt Paulson. He's in charge of the case. He was in court today, and I mentioned that I had met you. Of course, I never said anything about your overnight stay. It's none of his business."

Derek was squirming now. He couldn't seem to get away from the law in one way or another. This didn't bode well.

"Sure, I can talk to him, but I need to get on with my trip by tomorrow."

Fatal Rejection

"Oh, where are you heading?"

He figured it was time to start lying better. "I'm heading to Los Angeles to do more research for my next book. I'm just up here because I've always wanted to visit the city. But I must keep to my schedule or my publisher will have a fit."

"I can understand. Meet me in the jazz club around eight tonight, and I'll have Matt meet us there if it's okay with you."

"Works for me," he said, hoping she'd hang up.

"See you then," she said and hung up.

Great, he thought, this just keeps getting deeper. He should have just stayed in his room after he arrived or avoided people at all cost. He got back to his motel and went in. He opened the laptop. No mail. He figured he'd write his next chapter, even if it was made up. He couldn't get to any hookers here as the police were on alert for the bastard who was messing with his stay in Seattle. He hoped they would find him before he left, but with having to meet Sophia tonight, he knew it was useless to plan any attacks. And killing Sophia was definitely out of the question now.

About an hour later he finished his chapter and sent it off to Sarah. He still had a couple hours before he was to meet Sophia and the cop. He'd play it cool and calm. No one suspected him of anything. Besides, the murders occurred before he even got to Seattle, so he was safe.

He decided to get a little rest. The trip around the city had worn him down. Being a writer, he didn't get much exercise other than when he was killing people. He got a lot of exercise this last week, maybe too much. He lay on the bed after setting his alarm, thinking about what annoyances he would have tonight.

Meeting any more cops wasn't what he hoped for on this trip.

*

Chapter 24

Dave and Sarah finally had their breakfast together. On his way back from locking up the drunks, he had stopped at his apartment to get the ingredients for his pancakes, and Sarah thought they tasted divine. Had she latched onto a good man, she wondered? Was she going to wake up and find this was all a cruel dream? She munched on a slice of the apple he brought and watched him eat. He was graceful and carefully chewed his food.

Fatal Rejection

"Are you supposed to start work at any specific time?" she asked.

"A cop is always on duty, so we start when we get there. I usually try to maintain hours, but something always interrupts. As you saw this morning."

"At least you returned. I was worried that you didn't like what we did and would run away."

He looked at her and smiled. "No, I'm thoroughly happy with last night. I'll put a recommendation in the tourist guides, visit Sarah Keller for a good time."

She threw a piece of apple at him. He just sat, eating and grinning.

He had also brought a change of clothing, his uniform. He was dressed and said, "Now, I'm ready to go fight crime, or at least the drunks. Am I allowed to return?"

"If you don't, I'll tell everyone you're lousy in bed."

"They already know that. Or at least from what my ex spread around." He laughed, and she followed him out the front door on his way to his Bronco. They kissed again on the front porch then he forced himself to go to his car. She watched him drive out and sighed deeply. She suddenly felt a cold nose on her leg again and jumped.

"Damn it, dog, why do you keep doing that?" She led him off the porch to the back door and told him to get out. He disappeared again. She went to her desk where she saw the answering machine light blinking. "Crap, I forgot to check this last night." She pushed the button and listened. Denise's voice came over loud and clear. Sarah would need to call her. Then a second message came. She wondered why she hadn't heard the phone ring. Maybe while she was out front with Dave. It was Lois, of course, saying she'd call back shortly. Wonderful, Sarah thought. The phone rang causing Sarah to jump. She answered. It was Lois.

"Sarah, congratulations, I passed by this morning and saw Dave's car in the drive. How was it?"

"Lois, if you gossip about this, I'll never speak to you again."

"Sarah, I cross my heart I won't. I respect your privacy."

"Yes, it is my privacy which is why I'm not telling you anything about last night."

"Ah, leave it up to my imagination. Okay, glad you finally closed the deal."

Fatal Rejection

"Lois, I closed nothing…I mean, I didn't do any deal. It was a pleasant evening and that's all I'm saying, thank you." She hung up.

She returned her attentions to her desk and then looked up to the backyard. She saw Van Gogh running fast followed by two squirrels hot on his heels. She jumped up, ran to the door and called to him. He came shooting in the open door, and Sarah closed it before the squirrels could get in. They stood chattering at the door.

"What did you do? Are we going to have to move now because you offended the neighbors? I don't need battles with the local animals. They'll be cutting my tires next." Then she started laughing as the dog sat staring at the squirrels.

She went back to her desk and started up the computer. She had nothing from Harcourt. Good. There were two from Hal, and he sent a couple submissions from writers. She hated those, reading crappy manuscripts and having to reject them. In the past she would just send a standard rejection note, but Hal wanted a personal touch. Why? They wouldn't use the story, so why bother being polite?

She played with the files for a while, then her phone rang. She debated answering it but did. It was Denise.

"Denise, I'm sorry I didn't get back to you. I've been really busy." Yeah, having great sex. "I would like your other stories. Can you send them to me in an e-mail?"

"Sure, Sarah, that would work great. I have them all in a .doc file, if that's good for you?"

"Sure, send them and give me a few days, okay?"

"Great. I'll get them right out to you." She hung up, sounding happy. Sarah actually liked the girl who reminded her of when she was young. Enthusiastic and loved to write. But Sarah never did write a story worth showing people. She had no imagination for a good story, but she knew words and knew the correct way to write them. She worked hard and studied at a community college in Albany, getting her BA in literature. She worked for a couple smaller publishing firms then got her job at Scheuler Publishing. She had been there for almost eight years.

Her phone rang again. She made a mental note to call the phone company and get caller ID. Now she knew why Lois had the phone turned on for her before she moved in. Lois didn't get the caller ID so she wouldn't know if it was Lois. Clever woman.

She answered and was pleasantly surprised. It was Dave. "Well hello, Serpico."

"Who?" Dave asked.

Fatal Rejection

"A famous New York cop, undercover and the subject of a movie with Al Pacino. You never heard of him?"

"Now that you mention Al Pacino, I remember him. How are you feeling?"

"Great, but I could feel a lot better if you were here."

"Sorry, but it's a busy day. We've had a lot of tourists driving through. I've been handing out tickets right and left. It's how we pay my salary."

"Speaking of salary, are you going to be able to support me?"

"I hadn't thought of it. You could take up prostitution and I won't arrest you."

"Not my idea of a money maker, but I'd be one hell of a hooker," she said with a laugh. "Seriously, will I see you again?"

"You name the time, you got the place."

"Oh, I don't get to see your place? What's the matter? Will I find out you're a slob?"

"You can come to my place anytime. But be prepared to say hi to all the other apartment dwellers like the mayor and his wife."

"Oh, yes…maybe we should meet out here in the woods. You may come to my abode tonight if you are brave enough."

"What will you be wearing?"

"Perfume."

"I'll definitely see you later," he said and hung up.

She was getting a little warm from the conversation. She felt like when she was a teen and talking dirty on the phone to a boyfriend. As a matter of fact, he was the one who took her virginity then went off with another girl in school. Bastard.

She went out to get something to eat and fed the dog. This was getting routine. She needed a change. Maybe she could teach the dog to make lunch. No, he'd get hair in her sandwich. She started giggling. Must be the after effects of the drinks still in her system.

She decided now that she was finished with her work she would freshen up. She went to take another nice long bath. She was really pampering herself. She shut the dog out and did her ritual of preparing the tub.

An hour later she was dressed and ready for Dave. She was humming to herself, the Shania Twain song they danced to. She was happy.

She went to the computer and found the files that Denise had sent. She opened them and read. They were very good, very imaginative and well written for short stories. Sarah would have to encourage her to do a novel one day. But she didn't want to push her, just get her excited for now with what she had. The book world was changing. More writers and even some famous authors were starting to self-publish online. Amazon was the big place to sell your books. There were other avenues opening up, but the problem was that there were many people who couldn't write or could write but couldn't edit. They by-passed having someone edit their books so they put up inferior works. She wanted Denise to have her stories prepared properly, so she would help her.

She lost track of the time. It was almost seven when she heard the doorbell. She rushed to it but slowed as she got there. She didn't want to appear too eager. She opened the door and there stood her knight looking refreshed and handsome. He also had a bag.

"Crap, are you moving in?" She smiled as he came in.

"Just a few things to make our night pleasant. He went to the kitchen and pulled out a couple rubber containers, placing them on the island in the middle of the kitchen. She watched as he pulled a few more things from the bag. One was a vase with one rose which he handed to her.

"Only one rose?"

"Only one day we've been together." He smiled.

"I can't wait to see this vase after a year." She tried to look in the bag but he told her to go set the table in the dining area.

She felt giddy and went to do his bidding.

*

Chapter 25

Derek entered the jazz club again and saw Sophia sitting at the bar, looking conservatively dressed. He figured since a cop was coming, she wasn't going to be provocatively dressed. Derek went to her, and she latched on with a big kiss.

Fatal Rejection

"Wanted to get a good one in before Matt gets here. You up for a little exercise later?"

"I'm a little tired, but we'll see."

"Oh, tired of me already?"

"No, tired physically. I spent too much time running around today exploring this city. It's big."

"You could have called me. I would have given you a great tour."

"Thanks, but I'm kind of a private person. I like exploring on my own. That way I can enjoy getting into trouble."

The door to the club opened and in walked a large man in a suit. Derek thought this guy screamed, cop. The man saw Sophia and came to them.

"Matt, right on time. This is the famous Derek Harcourt. Derek this is Detective Matt Paulson."

"It's a pleasure meeting you, Mr. Harcourt. I've read your book," he said, as he extended his hand which Derek shook.

"Please call me Derek. Sophia tells me you want to pick my brain about serial killers."

"If you don't mind. We are at a standstill right now. Although the FBI has sent in a profiler, he's kind of a jerk and wants most of the attention. I'd like a different perspective from a man who has studied the NY Slasher."

"Do you suspect he might be back? He'd be rather old by now."

"Age doesn't slow murderers. They may get a little winded, but they still can kill," he said with a grin.

"I'm sure if the Slasher was back, he'd be in good shape."

"So shall we go to a table and talk?" the cop asked.

Derek helped Sophia off her stool, and they all went to a table on a side wall, secluded from the few other people in the club. It was still early. The jazz band hadn't even arrived yet.

After they were seated, the waitress took their drink orders and went off.

"So, Derek, what made you use the NY Slasher as a subject for your book?" Matt started off.

"I read about him years ago when he was still on his killing spree. I was out of circulation for about ten years, and he vanished during that time. I wanted to write a book about crime, and he was still fresh in the minds of people, so I went with him. I researched everything I could about him to get a feel for the man. It took a long while to get the book published, but he was still relevant."

"So do you think you know him, not personally, but know his method of killing?"

"Well, I have to admit, I'm no expert on him. I just used a lot of facts I gathered from books and wrote from what I read." Derek was trying to downplay his knowledge of serial killing. He needed to distance himself from the subject to throw off the cop.

The detective looked a little disappointed but continued, "Do you have any thoughts about the latest killings here in the city?"

The waitress returned with their drinks, handed them out and then went off.

Derek took a swallow of his drink and continued, "I haven't really been following it. I spent most my day sight-seeing around the city. Sorry."

"Well, the killer did tie his victims to a chair and slit their throats. It sounds like the Slasher's M.O."

"Maybe it's a copycat. Everything the Slasher did was in my book. Maybe the killer read it and is doing his kills the same."

"We thought of that, which is why I hoped you'd have some fact about him or his crimes that wasn't known by everyone else in the world."

"Sorry, just what you read in my book. Honestly, I don't claim to be an expert on serial killers or the Slasher. I'm an author who has no imagination, so I use facts from real life. I've never met the Slasher or talked to anyone who had any experience with him. I work from facts I gather that are available to anyone who wants to know about him. That's why I'm traveling the country to gather information about famous murders for my next book. I'm leaving in the morning to go down to LA to find out about their crime history."

The detective was disappointed. He smiled and said, "Well, it was nice of you to take the time to talk. I had hoped you might have something for us. So you have been traveling the country. Where have you been to?"

Derek had to be careful. He knew that the news was reporting similar murders along his route, so he had to divert his trip. "Well, I've been here and there. New Jersey, Kentucky, Missouri, Colorado, and finally made my way up here. This is mostly a pleasure trip, but I'm doing research along the way."

Fatal Rejection

"We've had reports that a killer similar to the Slasher has also been traveling again. It's good you haven't run into him. I wonder how he felt about your writing his story."

"Well, he's never contacted me so I wouldn't know. I hope he liked it so he wouldn't want to murder me," Derek said with a smile. Matt and Sophia laughed.

"Well, I won't take any more of your time, Derek. You two have a pleasant evening." He kissed Sophia on the cheek and shook Derek's hand again. He left out the door as Sophia put her hand on Derek's shoulder.

"Feel like visiting with me for a while upstairs?"

Derek was relieved that the cop didn't push him, so he was feeling better. "I'd like that."

They finished their drinks and left the club.

Sophia went off to work again the next morning. Derek lounged in the big comfortable bed after saying good-bye to her. He told her he would come back one day to see her again, but he knew he would never return. He dressed and left the apartment, finding his car in the parking lot on the side of the building, no ticket this time. He drove back to his motel and checked his e-mail.

He received the corrections for his made up story but nothing from his fans, Charles and Max. He felt a little miffed that they hadn't sent a message, but maybe that was a good thing. They were becoming pests with all their questions. He shut down the laptop and started packing. He had a very nice time in Seattle but he doubted he'd be back in the future. Brinnon was his next stop and hopefully his last before heading back to New York to his quiet life there. He wondered if he would be able to retire from his murders. The Slasher did it, so why not him? Of course, the Slasher could have been killed along his way, left in some unmarked grave. He never resurfaced in all these years, so maybe he was dead.

Derek packed his car and drove off toward the motel in Brinnon that he found on the Internet. The trip took him a long way around all the lakes and bays between Seattle and Brinnon. It took longer than he thought, although the trip was pleasant with all the scenery.

He was on the 101 North and drove slowly by Sarah's home. He could see a car in the drive, but he wasn't ready for a visit. He continued on through the town and found the Bayshore Motel just past the Brinnon General Store. He had called ahead for reservations and given them his Eugene name. He didn't want it known he was in the area after the murder was discovered.

Fatal Rejection

After he checked in, he went into his room. It was huge, clean and comfy. He put his things away and went to the door. He stood with it open, looking out at the sight of the Hood Canal. In the distance he could see Mt. Rainier. It was all so beautiful, he could see why Sarah moved there.

He knew there was no unsecured Wi-Fi in the area, but he had a wireless broadband adapter that he plugged in to get online. He used the device only when he couldn't hook up to Wi-Fi where he was staying. The provider limited his use of the device, so he didn't want to run out of time.

He did a quick check of his e-mail. There was none. He shut down the computer and decided to go eat. He went to his car and drove to the closest restaurant he was told about, the Halfway House.

He was seated and a bubbly girl came up and asked if he'd like some water.

"That would be nice," he replied as he looked at her name badge. It read Clara. She went off after giving him the menu. Derek thought that she was quite cute but a little too young for him. Besides, he didn't need or want much contact with the townspeople. He had a job to do, then he was out of there.

Clara returned with his water and took his order. She went off again as Derek stared out the window, admiring the area. His concentration was broken by the door opening. He turned to see who came in. It was a man in uniform, a sheriff's uniform. The sheriff stopped to talk to a couple people at a table, then he looked at Derek. The cop had very blue eyes.

Luckily, the sheriff went to the counter and ordered a coffee to go. He got his cup, said a few words to the woman at the counter, and left. Derek watched him drive away and breathed easier. He didn't want to be recognized after he took care of Sarah, so he thought it might be better to stay hidden.

His meal came and he ate. It was good for such a small restaurant. He finished and paid his bill then left the building quickly, trying not to be seen. He drove back down Highway 101 and slowly passed Sarah's house. He had found it on Google maps so he knew what to expect from the property. He drove past then turned around and went by it again. He passed the sheriff's car coming towards him, and in his rearview mirror he saw the sheriff pull into Sarah's drive. Now what did he want with her? Could this be a problem? He casually drove on and headed back to his motel, wondering if this was going to be another botched job.

He wasn't happy with the events of the last few days. He had no chance to murder anyone, and now a sheriff might be intruding on his last kill. Well, he wasn't going to let it upset him. He was primed for his final destination. He had waited years for it. He would go down in flames as long as he took Sarah with him.

Back in his motel, he relaxed in an easy chair and watched a little television. He would wait until dark before he attacked Sarah's home.

*

Chapter 26

The dinner that Dave prepared was delicious, Sarah thought. He included everything. The entree of roast beef and mashed potatoes was great. He brought non-alcoholic champagne and then he said he had a special dessert.

"Are you the dessert?" She smiled demurely.

"No, I have something better." He laughed then said, "Although, the two of us together would be a great desert. But I brought something else."

They finished the meal and he stood, bringing the bag over. He pulled out two éclairs. She giggled, and he bent to her to kiss her lips. She pulled his head and held it there for a moment longer. Then they dug into the pastries.

"I do have a dessert for you, too," she said.

"Later or now?"

She slowly opened the blouse she had on, and he saw the black lace teddy she was wearing. "Damn, now that beats the pastry."

They quickly finished the dessert and retired to the bedroom. Van Gogh figured he wasn't welcome so he passed out on the couch in the living room. Sarah didn't like him on the couch, but he wasn't allowed on the bed with them, so he got up there. When he heard her alarm sound in the morning, he would get off quickly.

In the morning the sun was streaming through the transoms above the huge windows in the living room. The curtains held back the sunlight, so the room was still fairly dark. The former owner had designed the window panes from floor to ceiling with transoms at the top that opened for air to get in. When the curtains were pulled back one could see all of the canal from above the property line to the lower end. It was a beautiful sight. Sarah had placed her desk facing the windows so she could look out at it. She also could see the animals wandering in her back yard, but with Van Gogh, the animals weren't around as much.

It was Monday morning. She usually hated Mondays, but Dave made mornings bearable. Sarah staggered out and to the kitchen. Van Gogh had vacated the couch when he heard the bedroom door open earlier when Dave slipped out to go to work. No breakfast that morning. He had to relieve Mike who pulled an all-nighter. She got a drink from the sink and smiled at the dog. "I'm sorry, puppy, I know you like to sleep with me, but you can't compete with the human person. It's a biological thing. Someday when Dave gets comfortable, maybe you can join us, but only to sleep."

She put the glass back on the counter and went to her desk. She didn't need to boot the computer. It was already on. Odd, she thought. There were a couple e-mails from New York and none from Harcourt. She was relieved. Maybe if she was going to be busy with being domestic, she could tell Harcourt to take his chapters elsewhere. It would be fine with her. He paid well, and it was under the table so she could use it as she saw fit. But having all the insurance money she did, she didn't really need his crap. Something to think about.

She went to take a quick shower and dressed for the day. Her dog was strangely absent. She wondered where he was off to. She went to the living room and was surprised to see the door to the backyard was open. She distinctly remembered locking it last night. She went to the door and stepped out. She called for Van Gogh, who came tearing out of the woods and up to her.

"How the hell did you get the door open?" she asked. Then she wondered if Dave might have opened it to let the dog out and forgot to close it. Nonsense, he was a cop and wouldn't go off leaving a door open. This worried her. She closed and locked the door and went to the phone. She called Dave's cell phone number and he came on.

"Hey, beautiful, you miss me already?" he said when he answered.

"Of course I do, but I have a question. Did you open the door from the living room to the back yard this morning?"

"No, I didn't. Why?"

"I got up and Van Gogh was gone. The door was wide open, and he was outside. I'm sure he didn't open it. At least I don't think he did. Can dogs unlock doors?"

"Not in my experience. Did you lock it last night?"

"Of course I did. When I locked it, I thought about letting the dog take one last run, but I wanted to get back to bed with you. I know it was locked, but this morning the door was wide open. I'm worried."

Fatal Rejection

"Well, don't be. Maybe the door wasn't totally closed. Van Gogh could have pushed on it and gone out."

"I hope that's the reason, but I am uneasy now. Do you think someone could have tried to get in, and the dog scared them away?"

"Well, if so, then Van Gogh earned his place in the house."

"Yes, he did. I'm not happy, but I'll let it go for now. Are you coming over tonight?"

"Boy, you are taking over my life."

"Yes, I am. I better see you tonight." She laughed and hung up. Then she stopped laughing. She was looking at the door and searching her memory to be sure she locked it last night. She was sure she did.

She shook it off. This was not something she liked, but she hoped there was a simple explanation for it.

~~*~~

Bob Moats

Derek smiled, thinking about his early morning trip to Sarah's home. He carefully unlocked the back door and opened it, leaving it open. He had been watching the house the night before and saw the sheriff coming to visit. He wasn't happy about it, but not much he could do. He knew he could make a false call for help and get him out of the area for a while so he could do what he had to do with Sarah. The dog was another problem, so he got some treats and took them with him. He was lucky. The dog slept through his break-in, proving he was stealthy enough to get in and out of a house even with a dog.

He had stood just outside the home and studied the layout. He needed to know what to expect from the house, since it was not a standard design. An octagon shaped house, very interesting. It had only three doors in or out—the front, the side, and the back where he had stood. The windows didn't open since they were huge panes of glass making up the back wall of the house facing the canal. The bedrooms were part of the back wall. They also had the windows so he could only get in from the three doors. He knew the back one was easy enough to open.

He left before Sarah got up. The sheriff had left earlier. He knew enough now to satisfy him. He went back to his motel to rest for the big encore, the reason he went to all this trouble to get out here.

Fatal Rejection

~~*~~

Sarah was busy working on a few manuscripts. She finished those, opened up Denise's stories and read them for a while. She enjoyed her writings and made a few corrections. Afterward she printed out the stories she thought were usable. She closed them down and decided to take a ride into town. She had been cooped up too long. She called for Van Gogh, and he came lumbering up looking half asleep.

"What are you so tired for, mutt? You slept all night, or I think you did." She thought about the door again and when it could have been opened. Maybe Van Gogh was out all night partying with the furry little animals. But not the squirrels, definitely not them. She smiled with the thought and got his leash.

She got her jacket and keys, then they went to the car. She drove up the highway and thought about visiting the sheriff's office to see where Dave worked. Maybe she should go to the restaurant, his second office. She went to the sheriff's office first and parked. She put the dog on his short leash and took him in the building. There were no signs saying no animals, so she didn't care. Besides, she had an in with the sheriff. She went around a corner to a desk and startled Dave.

"Well, this is pleasant. Are you out getting some air?"

"I just wanted a kiss from you." She saw there was no one in the office and leaned over the desk and kissed him. She heard a wolf whistle and turned her head to see a jail cell around another corner. There were two men locked up in it. She blushed.

"Shut up, you guys. This is my woman," Dave said.

Sarah smiled at being called his "woman." She would reward him for that later.

"Are you working all alone?" she asked.

"Yep, but that may change soon if the new budget is passed by the town. I can hire a new officer then."

"Good, more breaks for you."

"Yes, and no late night runs to haul in drunks."

"Good, nothing like being interrupted in the middle of late night fun."

"You are just a wild woman, aren't you? Anything new on the open door?"

"No, I distinctly remember locking the door. If you didn't open it and I didn't and the dog couldn't, how was it opened?"

"Well, if it happens again, I'll do a thorough investigation."

"You'd better. You wouldn't want to find me all hacked up by some killer, would you?"

*

Chapter 27

Derek was sitting in his car as he watched Sarah go into the sheriff's office. He assumed she had an affair going on with the man. Shame on her, he thought, so soon after her husband was murdered. Derek had hoped she would remain in mourning for her husband until he could get his chance to kill her. He didn't want her to forget the murders of her husband and the woman he was painting. He wanted her despondent and a broken woman, but this might be something better yet. He could play with her new feelings for this sheriff, really torment her. He had an idea, started his car and went back to his motel.

Back in his room he started up the laptop and sat to write out a chapter that he would send to Sarah later that day. He was so evil, he thought. He would send it to her even though it was not a good idea to reveal himself. But he didn't care at the moment, he just wanted revenge at all costs. He was fed up with the writing. It was starting to be too hard for him to bother with it, having to build a plot and define his characters and be precise with his words so no one would bitch about it. He was fed up with all the experts out there who put down his book for being inferior and poorly written. He just didn't want to finish this new book.

He was busy typing the story that would drive Sarah to the brink again. He loved it. He finished and re-read it again, making changes here and there to make it more gruesome. He saved the file, putting it aside to send later, waiting for the right time before he struck.

He turned on the television and saw a special report on how they caught the hooker killer in Seattle. He sat up and watched with great attention. The reporter was talking to a police official about how they broke the case.

The cop puffed out his chest and said, "Margot, we spent a great deal of time staking out the places where these women plied their trade. We often would have crack downs on the ladies of the night, but the next night they would be out in full force again. We did have undercover officers hanging around the street corners with backup officers watching from a safe distance. We got lucky. The perp solicited one of our officers, and after he left the area with her in his car, we pulled him over. He had in his possession the same items that our killer used to murder the other victims. We knew then that we had our killer."

The reporter pulled the microphone back and asked into it, "Is this the infamous NY Slasher that they say was possibly doing these murders?" She held the mic back to the officer.

"Oh no, Margot, he's too young to be the Slasher. The FBI says the Slasher would have to be in his sixties by now. Our perp is only in his thirties, but we have all the evidence to say he is the killer of the prostitutes in Seattle."

"So our streets are safe again to be out after dark?"

"Yes, Margot, but they always were safe, except for the hookers." He gave a little chuckle.

Pompous ass, Derek thought. He knew the streets were never safe for anyone. What with the crime rate up, drug deals gone bad, robberies for cash to buy drugs, no one was safe. He was happy that they caught the bastard. Maybe they wouldn't be looking more. They didn't say if he was a resident of Seattle or drifted in from out of town. He hoped they would pin his own murders across the country on this killer so they would drop all the investigations.

He shut off the television and decided to rest for his big night.

~~*~~

Dave waited until Mike came in to relieve him, then he, Sarah, and the dog left the building. Sarah put Van Gogh in the back of her car, and Dave got into the passenger seat.

"Now if you have to chase a criminal, I get to drive, right?" she asked.

"The town only has one patrol car for now, so I guess I would have to commandeer your vehicle," he said with a grin.

"Shall we go eat at the Halfway House?" she asked.

"Sounds good, if you don't mind being seen with me."

"I can stand it," she said as she drove to the restaurant.

They arrived and she parked. The lot wasn't very full so she relaxed wondering who they might run into. They went in, leaving Van Gogh to rest in the back of the car. Clara said hi to Dave and just smiled at Sarah. Jealous maybe, Sarah thought. They went to a booth and sat. Clara dropped off the menus and asked if they wanted water. She went off as Sarah leaned forward to Dave.

"I think the girl has a crush on you. I can tell by the way she looks at you."

"Sarah, I'm old enough to be her father, and maybe I am," he said with a sly grin while studying the menu.

"Oh, confession time. You slept with her mother?"

"Long ago. If she was my daughter, she'd be in her late twenties by now. So I don't worry. Besides, her father is a salesman for a local hardware store."

"How many other women in town have you slept with?"

"No more than three, and they are all married now and getting old."

"What does that say about you? Are you getting old?"

"You ask a lot of questions. Are you inter-viewing me for a job?"

"Yes, for a position in my bedroom. I think you've been honest, so you're hired."

"Great, when do I start?"

"Tonight, and the uniform is casual. Then you slip into nothing."

"I can handle that."

Clara returned with the water, took their orders, then went off.

Sarah and Dave sat talking until Sarah put her head low like she was avoiding someone.

"What's wrong?" Dave asked, then looked towards the door. Lois was entering. "You know she's going to find you so sit up and face the firing squad," he said with a laugh.

She glanced at him then sat up. Lois saw her and Dave and made a beeline to them.

"Crap," Sarah said under her breath. Dave was trying not to laugh.

"Sarah! Dave! How nice to see you two together," she said loudly.

"Lois, you don't have to yell. We're just having a bite to eat," Sarah replied.

191

Fatal Rejection

"And a bite later," Dave said under his breath. Sarah kicked him under the table.

"Well, it's good to see you two are getting friendly at least. My work is done here." She laughed, went to the counter and sat on a stool.

"I doubt she's done. She won't rest until we are married. You just watch."

Dave sat grinning. "You think it's funny?" Sarah asked.

"No, but I love watching you squirm." He laughed.

~~*~~

Derek woke and stood by the bed. He looked at the clock. It was five, and he wanted to go see what Sarah was up to. He went out to his car and drove back towards Sarah's house. He had found a good place to park his car earlier and went back there. Looking around, seeing no one, he walked to the edge of the cliff dropping down to the canal and went along the shore line to the back of Sarah's home. He came up to the fence at the cliff's edge behind her home and watched the house. There was no activity, which was good and yet not good. He moved behind the bushes towards the front. Her car was gone. He decided he would wait for her.

~~*~~

Dave's cell phone rang as they were eating their meal. He answered. "Hello?" He listened for a moment then said, "Shit. I'll be there shortly."

He shut the phone off and looked sadly at Sarah.

"You have to work?" she asked him.

"Mike stumbled off the porch of the office and broke his leg. Can you believe that? I have to take over for him. He was taken to the hospital by Virgil who was with him at the time. I'm sorry, but we'll have to have a rain check for our night. I'll be on all night."

"Damn, I bought two teddies for our meetings."

"Nice, but the first wasn't even on long enough."

"You could have let me wear it a bit longer. But you are such an animal. Oh well, I'll let Van Gogh sleep with me tonight."

"You are so cheap, sleeping with any man handy."

193

Fatal Rejection

She threw a French fry at him. "I'll take you back and go sadly back to my home." She pouted. Clara brought the bill and Dave paid. They went out to the car, and Sarah drove Dave back to his office. They kissed a bit in the car before he went in. She drove home.

~~*~~

Derek was sitting on a folding stool he had in his car when he finally saw her drive in. He watched from the bushes as she got out of the car and let Van Gogh run loose for a bit while she watched him. Derek didn't see the sheriff, so he breathed easier. The dog came up close to him, but Sarah called him back. Van Gogh stood looking in his direction. He was afraid the dog would give him away, but he ran off when Sarah called. Derek sat waiting for his opportunity. This was the night.

*

Chapter 28

After Sarah went in, Derek ran back to his car. He opened the laptop and booted it up. When the computer was ready, he plugged in the wireless adapter and hooked it up to the Internet. He pulled out the e-mail file he wanted to send and read it once more. He was happy with it, and, despite his apprehensions about sending this damning letter, he pushed the send link, and it went off to her. After it was gone, he closed down the laptop and went back to watch the house. He saw lights turning on all over the place. She was probably spooked by the door being opened that morning. He smiled at his prank.

He went around to the back of the house by the water, and from his hiding place he could see her sitting at her desk. She clicked the computer power button to turn it on and sat back to wait for it to start up. He watched her with hate in his heart. Had she typed his rejection letter from this computer? He watched with delight, breathing heavily, as she leaned forward to read her e-mails. Perhaps she had others, but she would eventually open up his mail and then she would be grabbed by terror.

~~*~~

Fatal Rejection

Sarah opened up the e-mails that came from her New York office and filed them in folders to be checked later. She saw the one from Harcourt and debated whether she wanted to open it or not. She was growing tired of his crap, and maybe she would tell him to bag it. The subject line of the e-mail said, "For Sarah, personal." This intrigued her, and she opened it. She read it and couldn't finish it. She had a look of horror on her face as she got half-way through the letter. She could not believe what she was reading.

She stood and looked at the windows. She went and closed the curtains quickly. The letter unnerved her enough to want to hide. When the room was safe from prying eyes she went to the phone on her desk to call Dave. She lifted the receiver and found the phone was dead. She ran to the kitchen and pulled at that phone. It was dead also.

She ran to her jacket where she had her cell phone and managed to call Dave. He came on and she was in a panic. "Dave! I need help!"

"Hey, girl, calm down. What's the matter?"

"Dave! I just got an e-mail from Harcourt, the author in New York I've been editing chapters for. I can't believe what he sent me."

"What?"

"He sent a chapter about the murder of my husband and my best friend Betsy."

"Why would he do that?"

"I don't know! He described the bedroom in great detail. He had to have been there, Dave! The police and the news never described the room. He had to have been there! He sent this to me, but why? Is he admitting to the murder? Are all his chapters he wrote about a killer murdering women and hookers real crimes he committed? Was he admitting to those, too? Dave, I'm frightened. You have to do something about this!"

"Well, he's in New York and right now it's about midnight there. I'll have to call in the morning to talk to the police out there about this. Don't worry, he can't hurt you. He is pulling something, and it will get him arrested. Don't worry."

"Dave, can't you come to sit with me tonight?"

"Baby, I'd love to, but right now I'm at the scene of a car accident on the 101. We have injuries and are waiting for an ambulance. I'll try to get there when I can, but I'm the only officer on duty. Mike is still in the hospital. Harcourt can't hurt you other than frightening you with this e-mail. We can take care of it in the morning, early. Okay?"

"Dave, the phones in the house are dead. What's that mean?"

"Well, this accident hit a telephone pole and it's down. Maybe that's the problem. Stop worrying."

She took a breath and said, "I'm not going to sleep. I don't have a gun, but I do have a carving knife somewhere in the boxes."

"Good, go dig it out and call me every hour so I'll know you're alright."

"Hell, I'm calling every half hour."

"Works for me. The ambulance is here, so I have to go. Talk later." He hung up. Sarah stood in the middle of the kitchen then went to the bedroom where her boxes were. She found one that said "Kitchen," opened it and dug in to find the big knife. She went back out of the room and nearly tripped over Van Gogh.

"Damn it, dog, go lie down." He put his head down and slunk off. "Van Gogh, I'm sorry, I'm a little upset right now. I need you to protect me," she said as she followed the dog into the living room. The dog turned and stood looking at her. "I'm sorry," she said in her nicest voice. He started wagging his tail, and she went to the couch, calling him over. She told him to come up next to her. He hesitated, probably wondering if it was a trick.

"Come on, puppy. I need you next to me, please." He jumped up and plopped down next to her. She reached over and picked up the remote for the television that sat in the room unused. She hardly watched television and didn't even know what was on the thing. She sat watching some show about a hospital full of crazy nurses and doctors. It was actually funny, and it was keeping her mind off killers.

~~*~~

Derek slowly came up behind the house. He found a crack in a curtain and could see Sarah sitting on the couch with the dog. He stifled a laugh at her bravado and went around to the side door where he worked the lock and opened the door. He left it open wide and then banged on the door, loud, so she would hear. The dog started barking, and he could hear him coming. He went quickly around to the back of the house again and looked into the crack in the curtain. He could see her standing in the living room holding tightly to the knife. He smiled and patted his knife in its sheath.

Fatal Rejection

~~*~~

Sarah's heart was beating loud enough to be heard by Dave, wherever he was. Van Gogh was still barking at the back, so she pulled herself up and went to see what had happened. She slowly went to the utility room with the knife out in front of her. She saw the side door was wide open. Her heart froze. She ran back into the kitchen to call Dave again. She got no response. Her battery was dead.

"Shit!!" she yelled, and went to the drawer in the kitchen to get the charger that she rarely brought out. She tried to plug it into the wall receptacle, but she was shaking so bad she couldn't get the plug in right. She finally got it in and plugged the phone into the cord to charge it. She tried to call out, but the battery was so dead it wouldn't work even on the charger. "Damn, phone, I'm changing carriers!"

She turned back to the open door and debated as to whether she should go back and lock it. She went down the hall to the utility room and peeked around the corner. The side door was still open. She burst into the room, jumped over Van Gogh, grabbed the door handle and pulled it shut. She reached down, threw the locking bolt at the middle of the door and ran out of the room.

Van Gogh followed her back to the living room. She came in and found the back door was wide open. She froze as someone stepped into the doorway. It was a man dressed in black. She almost swallowed her tongue trying to scream. The man rushed at her, but Van Gogh came up fast and attacked him. This gave Sarah enough time to run, but the dog was still there with the man. She turned in time to see the man grab the dog, lift him up over his head and toss the animal at a wall. Van Gogh hit the wall with such force that the thud could be heard by her. The dog fell to the ground and lay still.

"Nooo!" Sarah screamed. "You bastard!" she yelled at the man, but he came at her with something in his hand. She didn't know what it was, but he held it out front of him and fired it. Two wires came streaming from the thing as she realized in a moment of time that it was a Taser. She quickly ducked, and the wires whizzed over her head. She heard the man yell, "Shit," and he pulled another from his belt.

Sarah ran down the hallway towards the back of the house and into the utility room where she tried to open the door but forgot that she had pulled the locking latch and had to reach down to open it. By this time, the man had entered the room and she didn't have the door open yet. She had her back to the door. She wasn't able to open it before he could get to her. He just stood there with the damn stun gun pointing at her. He smiled and said, "Hello, Sarah, allow me to introduce myself. I'm Derek Harcourt, your husband's murderer and soon to be yours."

He was just starting to move towards her when Sarah saw a dark figure come up behind him, striking him in the head with some object. Derek looked stunned and went down to the floor.

Sarah was relieved, but who saved her?

*

Chapter 29

The man was in the shadows of the room. He was big and still had something in his hand that he used on Derek. He stood for a moment not moving.

"Thank you for saving me, whoever you are," she said. The man still didn't move. Sarah was still frightened. Then he came forward into the light. He was an older man, grey hair and gaunt face. She didn't know him.

"Don't be so relieved, Sarah. I just stopped Harcourt because I wanted to kill you for myself," he growled, his voice sounding gravely.

He reached down, picked up the stun gun and aimed it at Sarah. He pulled the trigger. Sarah had no place to go. The wires hit her, and everything went black.

Sarah awoke slowly, opening her eyes, but not moving. Her body hurt from the electric shock. She glanced around and saw something she didn't want to see. Derek was tied to one of her fancy wooden dining table chairs with plastic zip ties, duct tape on his mouth. He was still unconscious. They were in the living room, Harcourt in the middle of the room and Sarah on the floor by the couch. She didn't move a muscle. Then she heard the man moving around in the kitchen. He came back, and Sarah pretended she was still out. She peeked through her eyelids and watched the man go to Harcourt. He had in one hand Sarah's carving knife and in the other he had a glass of water which he threw at Harcourt's face.

Derek stirred and looked up at the man, eyes wide. The man leaned into him and said, "Hi, Derek. You don't know me formally, but I'm the man you made famous with your abominable book. Now you know? I'm the real NY Slasher, and I'm back! Just for you. You know me as Max Forbish, but that's not my real name. It's Max Draegon. No one knows me. I disappeared years ago when I got tired of murdering hookers. I loved murdering hookers. My mother was a hooker, and I murdered her, too. They all reminded me of my mother, so I killed them. You made such a show of my life, I just stayed in hiding. Your fucking book, did you ask if you could write about me? Did you? No, you just went ahead and did it. You screwed up all the facts and made a mockery out of me, you little pissant."

The Slasher walked around Derek a few times. Derek closed his eyes every time the Slasher went behind him, waiting for the knife he had in his hand to slit his throat. He didn't do it yet. How much torture would Derek stand? The Slasher played with him. He would look over to Sarah every so often to check on her. She was still out, he figured.

Sarah kept her eyes closed but would peek out to see what was going on. Luckily, the Slasher hadn't bound her so she was free to move if she had to. She waited for the right moment.

"I've been following you, Derek. You weren't all that clever, and you bragged a bit too much with your e-mails. I was both Max Forbish and Charles Weaver so I could play with you and get the info I needed to see what you were up to. You gave away too much about your trip, so I was able to do a little checking and found you. I joined up with you in Seattle since I lived close and followed you from there. I was in the Seattle jazz club watching you with that bimbo you fucked, and then I followed you here. I enjoyed stalking you to your destination. Oh, and I was the killer of the hookers in Seattle, but I framed that stupid drug addled creep for the murders. He was useless anyway, and the police needed a suspect."

"You were right, Derek. Google does help a criminal find out about his victims. I followed you to this place and your hiding spot in the woods. I stood behind you as you watched the house and followed you in when you went after the woman."

He went behind Derek and said, "I'm sorry. Am I talking too much? I just wanted you to know how I got here before you die." The Slasher grabbed Derek's head and pulled it back, dragging the carving knife across his throat. Blood gushed. He had his back to Sarah, so she made her move.

She got up as quietly as she could while Derek was making noises as his blood gushed out of him. Sarah was in the hallway when she heard footsteps behind her coming fast. She didn't look back, she just moved forward as fast as she could. She entered the open bedroom door, went through to her bed and around the other side. She turned for a moment and saw the Slasher at the door, just entering. She went through the bathroom connecting door and slammed it shut. She went into the other bedroom through the other door and slammed that shut. Luckily, the doors locked from the bedroom side, and she locked the door. She went to the door to the hallway and opened it, then went to the back of the room, behind a pile of boxes, and hid on the floor. She could hear the man crashing at the door until it gave. He reached through the splintered wood and unlocked the door. He came in, saw the open door and went to it and out. Sarah waited, listening for him, as he lumbered through the house.

Damn, she would have to remember to keep her phone charged. She wished she had it right now. She lay still waiting, then she looked up over the boxes. He was not around. She was closer to the back door from there so she decided to make a run for it out into the night. She went to the broken bathroom door again and slowly went through the room. She got to the other door to her bedroom and went through. She peeked into the hall and made a dash for the living room. She got to her desk when he suddenly appeared from the outside door. She went around the desk, hoping to ward him off. He came around it as she pulled the desk chair out, hoping to slow him.

He grabbed onto the chair, lifted it up high and tossed it to his right. It hit the window, shattering the huge plate glass pane. He stopped briefly when he heard the glass break then continued to chase Sarah out of the living room and into the front vestibule. She managed to open the front door and ran out into the dark.

She could hear him swearing about her escape. She didn't have her car keys, so she went into the woods. She could still hear him yelling.

"Sarah! We're far from help. I'll find you, be sure of that. If I don't find you tonight, your life will be a hell as I stalk you to kill!"

Bob Moats

Sarah was behind a bush in sight of the man. Her heart was pounding so hard, she thought it would burst. She could hear it pounding in her ears. She wondered if her cell phone was charged enough to call Dave, but that meant having to go back into the house. She heard the Slasher charging through the bushes away from her. She figured it was now or never. She quietly went through the bushes towards the house and ran to the front door. It was still open, making it easier to get in. She ran to the kitchen and to the charger, but the phone was missing! Damn, he must have taken it, she thought.

She heard his footsteps on the porch, so she ran back towards the utility room and hopefully out the side door. On her way she managed to grab her keys off the kitchen counter and hoped she could make it to the car. She burst through the side door and ran all the way around the building until she was in sight of her car. She ran full out towards it, but the Slasher came up from her right and got in front of her. He was too far to get her so she ran back towards the back of the house. Maybe she could jump the cliff of the canal and go down the shoreline to the neighbors. It was worth a try.

He was hot on her heels as she ran into the railing that guarded the ledge. She fell over it and collapsed on the ground, the breath knocked out of her. The Slasher came up and grabbed onto her shirt. He pulled her up and dragged her back to the house.

207

Fatal Rejection

He threw her down on the floor of the living room into Derek's blood. She tried not to be sick at the sight of him sitting there with his throat cut.

"Damn it, girl, you sure are a handful," he said as he grabbed her wrists and zip tied them together, then her ankles. She was hogtied on the floor as he came over her.

"I didn't want to kill you. I'm here only because Derek came here, and I wanted him. But you are a witness now, so I can't leave you alive. I'm sorry, it's Derek's fault, so when you meet him in wherever we go after we die, you can kick him in the balls."

She looked up at the man as he raised the knife to plunge into her. It was over, she thought. She regretted not telling Dave how she really felt about him, but she was going to be brave and go out without a whimper. He was bringing the knife down as she heard three loud blasts from a gun. The Slasher looked shocked and turned to face whoever shot him. He saw it was a sheriff. He tried to attack him, but Dave fired two more times, bringing him down. He dropped next to Sarah. She closed her eyes as his head was facing her, looking grotesque.

Dave ran to her. Pulling out his pocket knife, he cut her bonds. She grabbed on to him with all the strength she had left and sobbed loudly.

*

Chapter 30

Dave pulled Sarah up from the floor and helped her to the couch, sitting close to her while she held on. Her face was slightly cut and bloody from scratches she got running through the bushes. Dave pulled his handkerchief and wiped her tears and the blood.

"Oh, God, I'm so glad to see you," she said, still sobbing, putting her head on his chest. "How did you know I was in trouble?"

"The house alarms," Dave replied.

"Alarms, what alarms?" She looked up. "Lois never mentioned any alarms," she said, sniffling.

"The guy who built this place wasn't worried about crime, but he did build in a system of alarms. For fire, burglary or any trouble that would need our attention. When they moved out, the system was shut down only for the door alarms. We didn't want any false calls what with Lois showing the house and all to sell it. But there are sensors attached to all the windows to report if one is broken from a burglary or accident. There's a transmitter on the roof that sends an alarm signal to our office if help is needed. Virgil was in the office and saw the alarm go off. He called me, and I came out here to check on you." He looked at the space where the window previously was before the Slasher threw the chair into it and broke it.

"Damn, if I had known that, I would have broken a window myself. Dave, Harcourt was out here all this time. He must have sent the e-mail just before he attacked. I still don't know why he wanted to kill me or why he murdered..." She choked. Dave held her tighter. "He must have murdered all those other women." She looked up at him again. "The man you shot was the NY Slasher. He said he came to get rid of Harcourt. He didn't want to kill me, but I was a witness. You got here just in time."

"Just like in the movies, eh?" he said. He could hear her giggle a little as he held her closer.

Dave heard a noise at the front door and drew his revolver, pointing it towards the front of the house. He put it down when he saw it was Virgil coming in. He stopped at the archway to the living room.

"Hey, Dave, I got worried, so I came out to see if you needed any help." His eyes grew wider when he saw the body on the floor.

"Good, Virg. Do me a favor. Go out to the patrol car radio, call the state police and tell them to get up here quick and bring their crime scene people. I shot the NY Slasher, and the other body is a possible serial killer." He pointed to Harcourt still in the chair with his throat slit open wide.

Virgil saw the body. He turned pale, abruptly turned around and ran out of the house.

Dave laughed. "Good thing he's not a cop although I almost barfed at my first crime scene. Are you feeling any better?"

"No, I just want to get out of here and take my…oh God! Van Gogh!" She jumped up and went behind the couch where the dog lay still. Dave followed her.

"That bastard Harcourt threw Van Gogh at the wall. Do you think he's alright, Dave?"

Dave checked the dog and said, "I'm no vet, but he's at least breathing. He may just have had the wind knocked out of him."

Sarah tried to pick up the dog's head, and he stirred, opening his eyes. He made a huffing sound and tried to lick Sarah's hand. She laughed.

"I think we should take him to Doc James, the town vet, just to be sure." Dave picked up the dog and placed him on the couch. Van Gogh struggled to get up, and Sarah helped him to a sitting position. He was still huffing, but he seemed better.

Fatal Rejection

"Van Gogh went after Harcourt when he tried to attack me. He was a brave puppy, weren't you?" She nuzzled the dog as he tried to lick her.

Virgil came back and said, "I got hold of the state police. They said they'd be more than happy to come get the bodies. The officer said he'd call Tacoma and Seattle, too, and let them know you got the killer." Virgil looked at the bodies again and rushed out.

Dave laughed, then Sarah said, "I can't stay here, not with all that's happened here. There's too much blood everywhere just like back home in New York. I hate this. Can I come stay with you?"

"I know a crime scene clean-up company in Tacoma that can come in. They do wonders to make a place look normal. I'll call after the forensics people say it's okay. And yes, you can stay with me, if you don't mind greeting all the neighbors every day. It's a small apartment complex."

"I'll personally kiss the neighbors every day. I'm so glad to be alive. When he lifted that knife, I was sure it was the end. But my knight in shining armor came just in time," she said with a smile. Then she said, "I'm also going to strangle Lois for not telling me about the alarms. So please don't arrest me. It will be justified."

"I'll even help you. Now let's get you out of here. I'll have Virgil drive you and Van Gogh to the vet even though it's late. Emergency call, I'll tell him. I'll have to wait here for the others to show."

They stood. Dave lifted the dog and went to the front door. Virgil sat on the porch steps looking ill. He stood when they came out. "Virg, take Sarah and the dog to Doc James and apologize for the lateness, but he needs to check the dog."

"Sure, Dave, will do." He reached out for the dog and took him to his pick-up truck.

Sarah kissed Dave, and he said, "You'll need to come back here to talk to the police, but I'll handle most of it since it happened in my jurisdiction. But they can take it if they want. I'll see you later."

She went to Virgil's truck and got in. Dave watched them drive off and sat down on the steps to wait.

Two hours later Sarah was back, and the state police forensic people were running around collecting evidence. They deemed it a justified shooting by the sheriff rescuing Sarah from the killer, after it was all explained.

"This guy was really the NY Slasher?" asked the lead detective of Sarah.

Fatal Rejection

"That's what he told Derek Harcourt, the guy in the chair. Harcourt was an author who wrote about the Slasher, and he didn't like it," Sarah explained.

"Hey, yeah, I read that book. So this is the joker who wrote it? I didn't like the book. I guess the Slasher didn't either. I'm sorry you had to go through all this. After you fill out a formal report, then we'll be done with you."

"Sure. Just to put this to rest, Harcourt murdered my husband and a number of women. I have all his confessions on my computer. You can have them."

"Thanks. And thank you, Dave. We'll take it from here."

Sarah and Dave went out to the front porch again as the county medical examiner was hauling the two bodies out to the black van. They stood watching as Sarah leaned on Dave. "The vet is keeping Van Gogh overnight. He may have a rib or two broken. We can go see him in the morning."

"I'll call New York to find the investigating officer on your husband's case just to wrap it all up." Dave put his arm around her and said, "Shall we go home?" She smiled and said she'd like that.

Dave handed his card to the lead officer and told him to just lock up and call if he needed anything further. Dave went back to Sarah, led her to his patrol car, and they drove out.

The next week was busy with news trucks and reporters from all over the country flocking to Brinnon as the place where the NY Slasher met his match. They sort of mentioned Harcourt since his book was about the Slasher and he was also a serial killer in his own right. They never gave him a fancy name. Sarah was sure that would piss him off from the beyond.

~~*~~

A month later Sarah's house had been thoroughly cleaned and put up for sale. Lois was properly chastised for forgetting about the alarms, and she began another quest to put the house on the market. Sarah was happily staying in Dave's apartment until they could get a bigger house. All of Sarah's boxes were put in a storage unit, much to her delight.

She made it a point to greet the mayor and his wife every morning when she took Van Gogh for his walk.

"I understand your reluctance to keep the Carlson house, but you should celebrate the fact that you weren't murdered and that two killers were brought to a just end," Dave said, hoping to convince her to let them stay in the house, leaving the apartment.

"I just don't feel right there now. It's another crime scene and I'm tired of living in crime scenes. That's why I left New York. I don't want to leave Brinnon. I'm happy here, somewhere here, other than there."

He gave her a puzzled look. "You know what I mean," she said. "I just want to stay here with you."

"Fortunately, I do understand. Since the town voted to increase the police budget, giving me a raise, we can live in better surroundings. Lois told me yesterday that she had a cute home north of here, and it was priced to sell."

"We can look. Now go to work so I can start writing."

"Are you still going to write about the murders?"

"Yes, I'm tired of helping others with their stories, and Connie is going to help me write it all the way from New York. I'm telling my story. I still have all the e-mails Derek sent me so I can put them in the book. His publisher isn't going to even touch his second book now so I'll sort of do it."

"Fine. What are you going to call it?"

"It may have a little flavor of New York, so I decided to tentatively call it 'My Life by da Hood.'" She laughed.

He kissed her and said, "That'll put the Hood Canal on the map. You'll have all the 'homies' flocking here to see it. That's a great title."

*

THE END

Read a preview of the second book of the Fatal Series, "Fatal Departure"

Chapter 1

She crashed through the brambles that scratched her face and hands and tore her clothing. The monster was gaining fast. She stumbled on a rotten tree limb on the ground, catching herself. She ran on into the dark, foreboding woods, deeper than she had ever gone before, losing her sense of direction. She didn't care. The creature behind her was gaining, which was worse than being lost. Hearing the thing howling and snarling behind her made her move faster.

She tried to climb a tall embankment, pulling at limbs and roots, trying to get a foothold in the crumbling dirt. She felt a hand on her ankle pulling her back. She kicked and tried to pull away, but the hand held on. She was afraid to look back, to see the monster's face. She pulled herself up as the hand slipped its grip and she reached the top of the drop-off. She was in an open field, no hiding places. She kept running forward as she heard the fiend coming over the crest.

The field went on forever as she kept pace ahead of her pursuer. She was losing breath and getting dizzy. She wanted to sit down in the middle of the field. Exhausted, she sat down and gave up. As she sat, she looked back in tears as the shadowy figure came rushing up and stopped above her, holding the huge knife in its hand. She closed her eyes and waited. Her head was pulled back, and the knife slit her throat, draining the blood and life from her. She tried to scream but couldn't, then it finally escaped her mouth. She screamed loud and long.

"What the hell?" came a voice from her left. She woke to see Dave in bed next to her, sitting up. "Are you all right, babe?"

Sweat poured down Sarah's face as she tried to sit up. Dave helped and put his arm around her. "It's alright, you just had a bad dream."

"Oh, God. It was horrible. I was running and running, trying to escape from something. It had no form, just a dark shadow," she cried and turned to her live-in love, Sheriff Dave Chandler. "I'm not sure

218

which serial killer it was." She was talking about the serial killers that she fought off three months ago in her former house south of Brinnon, Washington. The killers were given a ticket to hell, and Sarah was safe.

She and Dave had lived in his apartment for about a month after her house was put up for sale. They looked at a small house that her friend and real estate agent, Lois Carter, showed them. It was a cute three bedroom house with a big fenced in yard that her dog Van Gogh could run in. She named the dog after the painter because the dog was missing part of one ear. Sarah's former husband who was murdered by one of the serial killers was an artist, and he liked Vincent Van Gogh.

"This is the second time you've had these dreams. Maybe you should see someone before they get worse," Dave suggested.

"I'm not seeing a shrink. I don't need a shrink. I'm not crazy."

"I didn't say you are crazy. You're not. But we know the reason you are having these dreams. You should at least give it a try. Maybe it can help you to get past the memory."

"Yeah, well, Brinnon doesn't have a shrink."

"Actually, there is a psychologist in town. She helps people with the stress of living in a small town." He laughed. "No, really, she's a great shrink, but don't call her that."

"Is she one of the three women you've slept with in your sordid past?" She smiled and slapped him on the arm, lying back and pulling him to her. She kissed him and grabbed his ass.

"Hey, I'm not cheap. So are you going to see her?"

"If I say no, will it affect any sex between us?"

"It may. I don't like you screaming in the night."

"You like my screaming when we have sex," she said with a smile.

"Yes, and you sound like a banshee in heat."

"Screw you."

"I hope so." He smiled, kissed her, then they went back to sleep.

Dave got up around seven and dressed to go to fight crime. Luckily there was not much crime in this normally quiet town other than all the reporters still pestering them about the killing of the serial murderers. They still hounded Sarah when she tried to go shopping or take Van Gogh to the vet to check his injuries from the attack by Harcourt. Dave and his deputies had threatened them with arrest, but they all claimed their rights as the press to tell the world about the incident.

Dave would force them to get back, and life went on. This morning he was ready to go out as he kissed Sarah, still in bed. "Don't lounge there all day now. I'll be checking." He laughed and went off. Sarah rolled over and looked at the clock. She looked down to see Van Gogh staring at her by the side of the bed.

"What do you want, food or a crap?" she asked. Van Gogh barked and wagged his tail. "Okay, wait." She pulled herself out of bed and sat on the edge. Van Gogh went to the door and looked impatient. "Okay, hold on."

She stood and put on a robe, following the dog to the back door. Van Gogh was bouncing around as she opened the door, and he ran out. "Don't take all day," she yelled.

Sarah dragged herself to the kitchen. She and Dave had remodeled it to be more user friendly towards Sarah. She was not a great cook, but Dave set up the kitchen to have all the appliances handy and the cupboards organized so she could quickly find anything she needed. Now the chore of fixing breakfast was on Sarah since Dave was usually off to work early.

Fatal Rejection

She wasn't fond of cooking, but she needed sustenance in the morning so she learned to survive. Dave taught her how to make the great pancakes he had mastered. It took her a while, but she learned and was even able to flip them without hitting the ceiling or the stove.

She let Van Gogh back in when she saw him bouncing at the back door and then fed him. She ambled back to the bedroom, showered and dressed to face the world.

What she wanted was a good cup of coffee from Starbucks, but the nearest was over 200 miles away so she brewed her own cup and took it to the living room. Dave had placed her desk by the big window so she could look out. Unfortunately it was not the great view she had in her last home. Back there she could look out and see the Hood Canal and the sea gulls sailing over the water. In this new home her view was of the long front yard, the main road into town and, across the road, a cemetery.

She shivered every time she looked at the cemetery, so she usually tried not to look that far. She was determined to plant trees along the front of the property to block the view.

She sat at the desk, placed the coffee cup on a cup warmer and turned it on. She started up the laptop that held the chapters for the book she was writing and took a sip of the coffee. It wasn't very tasty, but it provided her the needed caffeine to wake her up. The computer finally started up, and she reread the last chapter she wrote.

She sat back and looked over at Van Gogh where he sat next to her chair. His eyes went from her to the laptop and back. "Don't you start badgering me to write. I don't know how these writers can get the motivation to do this. I've been on this for weeks and only have eight chapters done."

Van Gogh made his usual huffing noise that he made when he was bored. "Hey, don't take that attitude with me. I'm going to write. I just need inspiration."

She looked out at the cemetery and shivered. "Okay, that helped. Now on to murder." She sat forward and started to tap away at the keyboard as Van Gogh went off to lie down by the couch.

All the incidents about the serial killers were still fresh in her mind. The e-mails she had from Harcourt basically confessing to the murders he committed helped. Hal, her former boss at the publishing company she worked for, said if the book was good, he'd consider taking a shot at it. She was happy and still had a good deal of money from the insurance on her late husband, so they wouldn't starve.

The house on the canal still hadn't sold, so technically she still owned it. She didn't want to live there after the murders in the living room. It was too creepy. Then she looked out the window. "Was that any creepier than living across from a cemetery?" she said to herself. Van Gogh lifted his head, stared and then went back to sleep.

She spent the next hour writing her story, trying to be as accurate as she could about what had happened. She cringed when she added the gruesome facts about the murders of all the book editors. She found out from the FBI who investigated Harcourt that he was killing editors and working his way across the country to Sarah. She also found out that he wanted to murder her because she rejected his manuscript years back. To carry a grudge all that time, he had to be a wacko, she thought.

She remembered how Harcourt sat in her living room with his throat slit open and shivered again. Then she looked up just as a hearse and a small procession passed on its way to the cemetery. Not a sight to see this early in the morning. "Maybe I should go back to bed," she said to Van Gogh. He just snorted and continued sleeping.

Continued in the book...

Bob Moats

The Jim Richards series of books by Bob Moats

(In Series Order)
Classmate Murders
Vegas Showgirl Murders
Dominatrix Murders
Mistress Murders
Bridezilla Murders
Magic Murders
Strip Club Murders
Made-for-TV Murders
Mystery Cruise Murders
Talk Show Murders
Sin City Murders
Black Widow Murders
Vegas Vigilante Murders
Area 51 Murders
Mortuary Murders
Hypnotic Murders
Sunshine State Murders
Blue Suede Murders
Honky Tonk Murders
Dark Carnival Murders
Lipstick Murders
Pasta Murders
Talent Show Murders
Shyster Murders
Campground Murders
Network Murders
Reunion Murders
Big Apple Murders
Kennel Murders
Trick or Treat Murders
Santa Murders
Wiseguy Murders

For a preview or to purchase a book, go to
http://murdernovels.com

www.ingramcontent.com/pod-product-compliance
Lightning Source LLC
Chambersburg PA
CBHW070814120626
46556CB00002B/494